FIVE ... H™

MICK MORRIS
MYTH SOLVER

#3 CHAMP...
A Wave of Terror!

written by K.B. Brege
illustrated by D. Brege

ISBN 13: 978-0-9774119-2-4
ISBN 10: 0-9774119-2-3

The trademark Five Ways to Finish® is registered in the U.S. Patent and Trademark Office.
Printed in the United States of America
First Printing Paperback edition – December 2006

Copyediting by Janice Pollard. Email: pollard_jan@yahoo.com

Special Acknowledgements to Mick, Katie, and Karl. Also, special thanks to Jennifer Zaenglein for her wealth of knowledge on Champ.

This book is dedicated to all of the teachers, librarians and media specialists of the world who continue to enlighten, entertain, inspire, guide and teach our children. Thank you!

Table of Contents

#3 CHAMP... A Wave of Terror!

Chapter One

I could hardly breathe! The fur was thick in my face; it felt like it was smothering me! I didn't know if I should move or not! As far as I could remember, we had left California and Bigfoot behind, so why was I being covered with fur? My nose was beginning to itch! Oh no! I was going to sneeze! I tried to hold it in, but it was no use!

"AHHHHH…AHHHH CHOO!" I sneezed hard, as Horace jumped off my bed!

"MEEOOWW!"

"Horace! Silly cat! You can't sleep on my face! I thought you were Bigfoot or something!" I said, trying to catch my breath.

I was so relieved to see I was in my very own bed. I had completely forgotten about getting home in the middle of the night and that my grandmother had been there waiting with Horace. The cat that thinks he's a person! He's the craziest cat; he demands attention whenever we're home. And was I ever glad to be home!

It had been a long trip back from California. We had to stop at a few events and sign autographs. Mom and Dad had to answer questions from the audience. These were events

the cable station, Uncover, had planned for our show, 'Myth Solvers.'

Well, I shouldn't say *our*...it's my mom and dad's show. But lots of people ask Nathan, Sissy and I to autograph their Myth Solver photographs, too. We always get people asking us if we saw any aliens or Bigfoot. I always try to dodge the question by answering with another question, like, "Do you think we saw Bigfoot?" They usually laugh and walk away, because I hate lying and telling someone that I didn't encounter any myths – when I did!

Sometimes these things were held in malls or at restaurant openings. The restaurant openings are always the

2

most fun – because they always make us stay and eat like kings!

It was great to be back home, though, even if it was for just a short stay. We had just enough time to re-pack, as the busy summer continued.

Now we were off to spend a couple of weeks at our next location – Lake Champlain. It's a long deep lake that runs in between New York and Vermont. They say a lake monster named Champ lives in the lake…little did we know we would be lucky if we lived through this myth!

Chapter Two

"Mick...you up?" Dad yelled. "Time to get a move on..."

Startled from my thoughts, I jumped out of bed and yelled, "I'm up!" I picked up Horace and headed downstairs.

"Good morning. Did you sleep well?" asked Mom, smiling. She was definitely the morning person of the household.

"Well, hello, Mr. Myth Solving Man!" said my grandmother.

"Grandma...uh hello...you know about my myth solving?!" I asked.

"Of course I know. I know everything about my grandson, don't I? So, tell me all about your trip..." she replied.

"Oh...you mean about the trip..." I stuttered. For a minute my brain went crazy thinking my parents had found something out! I breathed a sigh of relief and shook it off. I told her all about the last two missions, leaving out a few particulars – like the fact that we had run into real aliens and discovered Bigfoot!

I did give her some details, the kind that most grandmothers like to hear. Like how much I enjoyed the clay she had bought for me to take on the trip.

Mom and Dad were busy restocking the Myth Mobile – the giant recreational vehicle we all traveled in, except for the crew and equipment. On this trip it would be the whole gang; even my Aunt Marisa would be joining us. Which I thought was great, because it would mean Sissy would spend more time with her mother and maybe less time with me.

Although, I couldn't be too hard on her – because as girlie-girl as she was, she did manage to get us out of quite a few hair-raising situations on the last few missions.

But little did I know that what was looming in our future would be totally more hair-raising and frightening than anything we had already encountered!

Chapter Three

I could hear people coming into the house, it was like a party! It felt really good and safe being in our own home with the crew and relatives. This time everyone was excited that we were taking some vacation time, mixed in with the filming. We were all going to stay in rented cabins in Port Henry, New York, on Lake Champlain.

Lake Champlain is a freshwater lake with lots of little coves and inlets. It is extremely similar in comparison to the Loch Ness in Scotland.

Now this is really strange to me because Loch Ness and Lake Champlain both claim to have lake monsters. The lake monsters even look the same in photographs. Only the Loch Ness monster, Nessie, has been around for thousands of years, and Lake Champlain's monster, Champ, is fairly new. But the United States is new compared to Scotland, so that's not saying much.

Now as far as aliens and Bigfoot, I had no doubts before we went on our expeditions and filming that they existed, but a lake monster; that seemed pretty ridiculous to me. I was just about finished packing and was putting my last few myth solving devices in my backpack when Nathan walked in to my room.

"What is up?" asked Nathan holding out his hand for our secret handshake.

"Dude! When did you get here?" I asked.

"Just now! My dad is downstairs. What a summer, huh?" asked Nathan.

Nathan is my best friend, and he is the director – Mr. Juarez's son. Nathan lives in Los Angeles, California, so he was much closer to home after the last mission. The cool thing is that when we are out of school, we both get to go on these totally awesome trips.

Nathan is like the total brainiac, really into technology, computers, and stuff like that. He even reads all the latest hi-tech magazines cover to cover.

Nathan proceeded to tell me how excited he was about this trip! He had his dad stop at a bookstore on the way to the airport so he could get a book about lake monsters. He proceeded to dig it out of his backpack to show me; while I told him the few things I knew about Champ.

"I read that Champ has been around for hundreds of years and that he was possibly first discovered by the French explorer Samuel de Champlain in 1609. That the lake is so big it could hold Loc Ness or Champ-type serpents!" I stated.

"Yeah, and did you know there have been hundreds of sightings ever since then, and there's even a famous photograph..," continued Nathan. We were deep into our discussion about Champ when…

"Don't you know that photographs can be retouched?" a familiar voice blurted out from my doorway.

As I looked up, I saw the monster had returned! There she was in her full head-to-toe pink outfit, complete with a pink visor and pink socks! Yuck!

"Oh, hey Sissy…" I groaned. And I knew this was going to be a very long trip.

Chapter Four

Nancy Boyd was walking toward Main Street in Port Henry, New York. She was on her way to the bakery to pick up some bread for her mother. As she walked by herself,

she was startled when the bushes next to her began to shake.

Instantly, two figures jumped out in front of her and two behind her!

"Champ, Champ is Nancy's only friend! He will be the death of her in the end...Champ, Champ is Nancy's only friend! He will be the death of her in the end!!!" The group chanted loudly as they surrounded her. Nancy tried to push her way through them but they only tightened the circle around her.

"Let me out of here!" she yelled.

But they just chanted louder as the circle got tighter. Suddenly, there was screaming behind them! It was old lady Irma who had come out on her front porch with her broom!

"Leave her alone you nasty little pukes!" Irma hollered at the top of her lungs.

Immediately, the gang scattered away. Nancy stood there for a second in shock, wiping her tears and straightening her clothes. When she turned to face the woman and thank her, old lady Irma was already shutting the front door to her spooky old house. As it slammed shut, Nancy pulled herself together and carefully began walking toward town again.

She hated those kids who always tormented her, every last one of them! She knew hate was a strong word, but she couldn't stand how they teased her all the time.

Why couldn't they believe her? Nobody would play with her, just because she told people she had seen Champ. But she had! And what she couldn't figure out was why nobody else had seen him. Nancy knew for a fact that she saw what she saw, an enormous long-necked, scary dinosaur-looking creature! And she had seen him more than once in Bulwagga Bay. She had seen him at least eight times, maybe ten! She couldn't keep track anymore. But she would never change her story, because it was the truth!

Chapter Five

"Good morning, Nancy," said Mrs. Kordell, smiling.

"Hello," Nancy replied sullenly.

"What, no smiles? Not happy today?" asked Mrs. Kordell, who owned the local bakery. She was a young, thin, pretty woman with long dark hair. She had relocated to Port Henry from Manhattan five years ago with her husband to open up the bakery. People in town said she and her husband used to be big time journalists – like famous, and they had traveled the world.

But they hated the crazy life they led, so they moved to the small town of Port Henry to lead a quieter life. They even bought a big old farmhouse up on a hill and had several llamas as pets. Mrs. Kordell had invited Nancy over to visit before, and Nancy loved playing with the llamas. Nancy liked the Kordells so much that she even had the nerve to tell Mrs. Kordell about the Champ sightings, and Mrs. Kordell believed her!

"I'm just here to pick up some bread for Mom," said Nancy.

"Oh, I see. You look like you aren't having the best day," said Mrs. Kordell.

"People just bug me sometimes," replied Nancy.

"Oh, I can relate to that, but I find the best cure for nasty people is one of my fresh-baked donuts, don't you agree?" asked Mrs. Kordell, as she leaned over the counter and handed Nancy a delicious, freshly-baked, gooey donut.

"Thank you. Anything new around this miserable old town?" grumbled Nancy, while paying for the bread.

"Well, as a matter of fact, yes! I couldn't wait to tell you about it! Did you happen to see the poster about the cable show coming to this miserable old town?" asked Mrs. Kordell, smiling. "The posters are in all the store windows."

"I'll take a look," said Nancy, and instantly hated herself for lying to Mrs. Kordell. She had lied because all a cable show coming to town meant to her was that she would be an outcast. All the cool kids – well, the kids who *thought* they were cool, would be involved. And, once again, she would be left out.

As Nancy left the bakery, Mrs. Kordell called out, "Don't forget to look at the posters! There's one right there in my window!"

The bakery screen door slammed shut and, just as Nancy turned to leave, the bright purple poster in the window caught the corner of her eye and she couldn't pull herself away.

Port Henry

is proud to announce that

The Uncover Cable Station

and the exciting

MYth Solver Show

Will be coming to Lake Champlain this Saturday!!!

Join the fun!

Saturday! Saturday! Today was Saturday! Nancy's heart was beating so hard it was about to pop out of her chest! She couldn't believe her eyes! This was what she had been waiting for! The Myth Solver show would be right in her own hometown! This was not just any old cable show! This would be her chance to prove to the world that Champ existed! Then nobody could make fun of her anymore! They were coming to little Port Henry!

But what she didn't know was that, at some point in the dark scary waters of Lake Champlain – Champ would be coming for her!

Chapter Six

"Mick. Nathan. Is this soooo totally cool?" asked Sissy.

"It's just another myth solving mission…" I replied, trying to sound calm while continuing to pack.

"Not that! My new outfit!" Sissy squealed.

"Oh, uh, yeah…it's beee-yooo-tee-fulll!" I exclaimed.

"Can I borrow it?" asked Nathan, and we both immediately broke out into total laughter.

"Fine, fine. But I am just trying to get my mind off the fact that I don't think I can handle another myth solving mission! I mean…we've been totally lucky the last two times – but when I think of the things that could've happened…" Sissy whined.

"Well, Sissy, for starters, you aren't supposed to think about it – I mean you shouldn't try to think to begin with, so that's your first mistake," I laughed.

"Yeah, consider the fact that you are one of the only humans on the planet to have actually run into an alien, or Bigfoot! Cryptozoologically speaking…" Nathan continued.

"Crypto-what-huh? Just what are you blabbering on about?" asked Sissy, who was now looking totally confused.

"He's talking about the science of cryptozoology. It's the study of…"

"And crypto stands for..." a familiar voice continued. I couldn't believe my eyes! It was Dennis Hinkelson standing right in my room!

"Dennis!" I said as I jumped up and ran over to give him a high five.

"Hey, kids! So what's the big secret here? You know I am the guy to tell about your wacky adventures," grinned Dennis.

We told Dennis about our fun, along with some of the scary stuff – like the freaks at the fair and about going on the Bigfoot search, but nothing about actually meeting real aliens or Bigfoot. We were afraid he would think we were either crazy, or worse than that, he might tell our parents. That was a fate I couldn't handle because our myth solving missions would end! Not knowing just how close we would get to the end of our lives in Port Henry!

Chapter Seven

As we all sat in a circle on the floor, we were laughing and talking about our past adventures and the creepy people we had met, like Uncle Buckey. Everything was going fine until I mentioned our plan of finding Champ.

Dennis immediately froze and shrugged his shoulders – almost as if he had a chill run up and down his spine. He then quickly stood up.

"You know, Mick, and Sissy and Nathan," he said in a very serious tone, "it's one thing to hunt for these creatures when you are near the camp and on dry land…but it's a totally different thing when you are out on treacherous, unknown waters that are extremely deep and dark. That lake is very, very dangerous! There are lots of hidden coves and inlets that are mysterious! There have been mysteries about Lake Champlain for over two hundred years. This mission is one even I am worried about. I'm warning you kids to be careful!" We all looked at one another fearfully as we nodded and Dennis abruptly left the room.

It was clearly visible he was shook up. The one thing that had me worried was, for starters, I had never seen Dennis get scared – about anything. Nor did he ever give us any kind of warnings. And even more frightening was Dennis had grown up in the Burlington, Vermont, area, which was just on the other side of Lake Champlain! We knew he was serious, but there was something more to it than that…it was almost as if Dennis himself had encountered Champ…and it was something we would find out soon enough!

Chapter Eight

Nancy tried as hard as she could to contain herself when she got home. But she felt like she was popping out of her skin, she was so excited! The minute she got in she handed her mom the bread as calmly as possible – not wanting to let on how excited she was. Then she went straight to her room and locked the door.

She quickly moved her nightstand, slid her bed over, and rolled up her rug. She quietly tapped her loose floorboard. It popped up and she gently removed it from the floor. Then she reached her hand into the dark opening and pulled out her secret old brown leather suitcase. It was taped on the sides it was so old, but it held some of her most precious secrets.

She took off her necklace and used the key on it to unlock the old brass lock and carefully opened it up. Inside was more information than anyone could ever imagine about Champ; books, papers, and even her own photos Nancy had taken of Champ. Things she had bought from stores or had her mother order for her on the Internet. It was Nancy's prized collection.

That was before everyone had started making fun of her, when her parents had decided she had taken it just a bit too far. So she hid her secret stash just to make sure no one would ever think of getting into it.

After digging through the suitcase, Nancy found her Myth Solver phone book she had gotten at a store, then quickly found the number she needed.

She went to her phone, gently picked it up and clicked it on. She was relieved to find out nobody else was using the phone. As she breathed a sigh of relief, she carefully punched in the numbers to somewhere she was never, ever allowed to call again…the mayor's office.

Chapter Nine

She had to disguise her voice, since they, too, thought she was a little crazy. In fact, since she had called so many times with Champ sightings and information about the lake monster, the mayor's office would no longer take her calls.

"Hello, it's a beautiful day in Port Henry. Lucille Dillwater speaking. How may I help you?" said the familiar secretary's voice.

"Eh-hem...I wonder if you could give me some information as to where the Myth Solver show will be staying?" asked Nancy in a fake deep voice.

"And who might this be inquiring?" asked Mrs. Dillwater.

"Uh, who, um...well, this is the New York Times calling from Manhattan," Nancy replied, proud that she had used her quick thinking improvisational skills.

"Oh my, well, yes...you need to talk to Mayor Roland...uh...let me get him right away!" said Mrs. Dillwater.

"NO! I mean, uh, no, that's not necessary. He's a busy man, I think, and we will talk to him when we get there – I just need to know where the crew will be staying, please," said Nancy, trying as hard as she could to control her shaking voice.

"Oh, well…alright. I happen to know they will be staying at the Pine Lake Resort cabins – why, I booked the reservation for them myself!" said Mrs. Dillwater.

"Awesome!" squealed Nancy in her regular voice, then quickly disguised it again. "I mean, that is, well, great! Thank you!" said Nancy as she hung up the phone.

Nancy was thrilled! The cabins were just down the road and up around the bend on an inlet, not far from her home. She quickly packed her proudest possession, her Myth Solver backpack her grandfather had bought for her years ago. Before…

BAM BAM BAM!!! Nancy jumped out of her skin as somebody pounded on her bedroom door. She slowly opened it only to see her younger brother, Tommy, holding out his hand.

"Gimme ten bucks or I'll tell Mom and Dad you called the mayor's office!" he snickered.

"You're an idiot!" snapped Nancy, as she tried with all of her might to push the door closed. But her brother only pushed harder.

"I'm not kidding…I know you called the mayor's office again!" yelled her brother.

"Freak…slimy little freak!" said Nancy, as she dug in her pocket and slapped her last ten dollar bill in his hand.

"Takes one to know one!" her brother laughed, "which is why you look like a sea serpent!"

"That doesn't even make sense!" said Nancy, as she slammed the bedroom door in his face.

It wasn't until later that day that Nancy found out the whole town was getting ready for a huge Myth Solver show welcome party and everyone was invited. She started to feel very strange and was surprised that her excitement was gone. She had a nervous feeling in the pit of her stomach. A feeling like something terrifying was about to happen...

Chapter Ten

The trip to Lake Champlain was only a fraction as long as the last drive. It was getting dark, so we were thrilled when the Myth Mobile pulled to a stop and Lenny announced that we had arrived! Lenny was our regular driver and he was happy to be back on a show.

Plus, it gave Uncle Hayden, who drove on the last two trips, a chance to enjoy this trip as a vacation with his family. We unbuckled and got up to gather our gear. Within seconds the Myth Solver bus with the show equipment and crew pulled up next to us.

Uncle Hayden and Dad told everyone to sit tight while they went to the office to find our cabins and check in. We picked up our games, books and magazines, then piled our backpacks and suitcases together.

There was a street light in front of the office and light coming from inside the office cabin, and a barn to the other side of the property that looked like it was lit up inside.

But on the lake side it was pitch black outside, except for the bright blue glow of the moon over the lake.

We could see it looked like the cabins lined some sort of bluff that dropped down to the huge black lake. I went to the window on the lake side and slid it open.

"That's gotta be Lake Champlain," I said, as Sissy and Nathan came over to look. As we peered out the open window, Sissy asked, "What's that splashing sound?"

"What sound?" I asked.

"That splashing sound…can't you hear it? Listen, it's coming from right out there, in the middle of the lake! I bet it's the lake monster!" said Sissy excitedly. At that very moment a huge wave of water splashed into the window of the Myth Mobile!

Chapter Eleven

Sissy screamed as Nathan and I flew backwards.

"What? What happened?" asked Mom, as she and Aunt Marisa came out from the kitchen.

"The lake monster!!!" Sissy screamed at the top of her lungs. "It was right out there! I heard it and then the next thing I knew it splashed water into the Myth Mobile and all over us!"

At that exact moment we heard massive laughter coming from outside of the Myth Mobile! Dennis, Mr. Juarez, and Brett, the sound man, popped their heads up from the side of the Myth Mobile while they all held up big Super Wet Blaster squirt guns to the window.

"Ok, that was not funny! Not funny at all!" griped Sissy, which made everyone laugh even harder. Just then, Dad and Uncle Hayden came back in.

"All set! Ten cabins, enough for all of us," said Dad.

"Can Nathan and I bunk together?" I asked.

"If it's okay with his father," Mom answered.

"Can I, Dad?" Nathan yelled out the window to his father.

"Fine with me, but always let me know where you are at."

"That's just no fair! I never have a friend to bunk with," cried Sissy.

"Well, you have me…" said Aunt Marisa. As Sissy went and hugged her.

Mr. Juarez, Dennis and James gave each one of us the giant squirt guns. We thanked them, gathered up our stuff, then Nathan and I ran as fast as we could to the end cabin. It was the one that was closest to the sandy bluff.

As we circled around to the door, I looked out over the lake and could've sworn I saw huge black bumps on the lake slowly go under water. It was late; my mind must've been playing tricks on me.

Chapter Twelve

As Nathan and I walked into the dark, musty-smelling cabin, shivers went up and down my spine. There was something spooky about the whole place. Just the thought that directly behind the cabin and down the sandy bluff was such an enormous body of dark black water – deep black water. Where possibly a sea serpent, lake monster type of creature lurked.

I flicked on the light switch and we could see the pine paneled room had two twin beds with plaid blankets and a pine dresser. There was an ancient mirror hanging over it and in the corner was a tiny bathroom and closet.

"Okay, this is what I call a cabin!" exclaimed Nathan. "Which bed do you want?"

"I'll take the one closest to the lake," I replied.

"Okay by me!" said Nathan as we both began to unpack our gear. It was getting late and we hadn't had dinner yet when there was a knock on the door, and then it opened.

"Dinner in the mess hall…" said Dad, as he came in eyeing our cabin and nodding. "Pretty much the same as ours. C'mon, they are putting on a small welcome dinner for us."

We left the cabin. The crew, Mom, Sissy, Uncle Hayden, Aunt Marisa, Mom and Nathan's dad were waiting outside. Dad introduced everyone to Mr. LaFave, the owner of Pine Lake Resort.

"Oh, please, call me Greg. I hope you people are hungry, the local folks are so happy to have you here that they wanted to show their hospitality," he said, as he walked up to a big brass bell and rang it.

When we approached the big barn he opened the large door and we walked inside. This was anything but a small welcome dinner! The place was completely lit up and packed with people. There were long tables decorated with red and white checkered tablecloths and lining the sides of the barn were tables covered with mounds of delicious food. It smelled awesome!

Straight ahead on a stage was a band that started playing the minute we all walked in. Then a short portly man with gray hair in a tweed suit walked up to the stage holding an enormous gold key with a big red ribbon. He motioned for the band to stop playing but they apparently didn't know what he meant and they played even louder. He waved his hands vigorously in the air and the band finally stopped.

He cleared his throat and leaned into the microphone, and instantly there was a huge squeal of feedback. He tapped the microphone again while a band member rushed up to adjust it.

"I am Mayor Roland, and we are happy to welcome you to Port Henry, New York. May I be the first to present you with a key to our fair city?" said Mayor Roland.

We all made our way to the front of the stage as Mom and Dad went up onstage to accept the enormous key.

But something felt really strange, almost as if someone was staring at me.

Chapter Thirteen

I slowly looked around. Then to my left I could see a girl with bangs and curly brown hair just glaring at me. She had piercing eyes – the kind you can feel burning a hole right through you. I looked away for a few seconds and then turned back again, only to see her still staring at me! I nudged Nathan.

"Nathan," I whispered. "Don't look now, but is that girl over there with the curly hair still staring at me?"

Nathan, of course, didn't listen and looked all over the room, until his eyes met with the girl.

"Uh yeah, totally!" said Nathan. The girl must've caught on that we had both seen her because when I looked back again she had disappeared in the crowd.

"That's weird," I said.

"What's weird? What's weird? This place? I actually think it's kind of quaint!" giggled Sissy as she popped up next to us. "It's just like the kind of small towns you see in the movies!" Again Sissy was way overdressed, like she was going to a prom or something.

"Uh, that's not what we're talking about, eavesdropper! And where did you think you were going?" I asked, as I stared at her with the most disgusted face I could muster up.

"To a party, which you obviously have no knowledge how to dress for!" barked Sissy.

Nathan and I rolled our eyes as she bounced away. We all found our seats to sit down and eat. Not knowing that as hungry as we were there was something lurking outside that was far hungrier than we were!

Chapter Fourteen

While we were eating, someone came up behind me and quickly dropped a note right over my head. It fell directly into my lap – but when I turned to see who did it, there was only the back of the strange girl who had been staring at me, running away. I slowly opened the note and read it.

Dear Mick Morris,

I am so glad you are here! I have to talk to you in private! I have seen Champ! More times than I can remember. I even know the areas where you can find him! Meet me in the back of your cabin at the bottom of the bluff after the party.

A fellow cryptozoologist,
Nancy Boyd

"What do you make of this?" I asked Nathan, as I slid him the note under the table. But the second he finished reading it, tons of local kids came over to introduce themselves, but not the mysterious girl named Nancy.

We all talked about Champ, but it seemed like none of the locals believed in the lake monster. They said their parents had always said it was a hoax and the only people who believed in Champ were a few crazy people. I asked them about the famous photograph and about the fact that people had claimed to see Champ for over two hundred years.

"Yeah, and you even have a 'Champ Day.'" I stated.

"We sure do. Nice to meet you, Mick Morris. My name is Tommy Stadler," said a friendly blond kid who came through the crowd. "My dad owns the general store and he is a big promoter of Champ Day. But he says it's only to draw in tourists."

"Oh, I see…" I answered.

"Ask them if they know that Nancy girl," prompted Nathan as he elbowed me.

"Uh, yeah…do any of you guys know a girl named Nancy?" I asked carefully.

Immediately, they all rolled their eyes and laughed. They called her crazy and said she liked to exaggerate. That every time there was a log floating on the lake Nancy would tell everyone it was Champ.

But something inside me told me there was more to it.

Chapter Fifteen

The party ended at 11:30 p.m. As we left, we shook hands with just about everybody there. We thanked the mayor, the city hall staff, and all the kind people while we said goodnight.

When we walked out of the giant barn one of the kids yelled, "Be careful not to get eaten by Champ!" and the rest of the townspeople who were leaving began to laugh.

We walked back across the large gravel lot to our cabins. It was dark outside except for the single street light on a pole in the middle of the lot and the eerie blue glow of the moon bouncing off the lake. By now we were feeling pretty tired.

"Get a good night's sleep, boys!" said Mom.

"We will, I promise. We're pooped!" I replied, as we reached the door to our tiny cabin. I stood at the door for a moment thinking.

"What's wrong?" asked Nathan from behind me, sounding puzzled.

"Did you leave the door open?" I asked.

"No," said Nathan.

"Look, it's ajar," I said.

The door to our cabin was slightly open!

"Hello? Who's in there?" I said, as I pushed the door open the rest of the way.

"Maybe we should get our parents," said Nathan.

"Anyone in there?" I asked again.

We could see the creepy, eerie glow from the moon that lit the room from the lakeside window. There was a spooky silence as I put my hand inside the door and groped for the light switch. I flicked it on. As we peered inside we could see that everything appeared to be in order.

We crept in very slowly and quietly, checking behind the door in the small closet, bathroom and under the beds. Then as Nathan shut the door behind us – we saw it! It was straight ahead of us!

Chapter Sixteen

On our mirror, written in blood red…

You must
believe me…
Don't Listen
to them.
Meet me as
      Planned.
I can Show you
where CHAMP is!!

nancy

"Okay…that's really weird! This girl is really starting to give me the creeps!" said Nathan.

"Awww, I think she's harmless," I answered as I walked up to the mirror and touched the writing. "It's just red lipstick anyway."

"I don't know, Mick…anyone who breaks into someone's cabin and writes in red lipstick on a mirror is pretty weird if you ask me!" said Nathan.

"That, or desperate," I replied as I cleaned off the mirror.

"Yeah, but what bothers me about this whole Champ thing is how few people have seen it," said Nathan.

"Maybe they just don't know where to look," I replied. As I got ready for bed I emptied my pockets on the dresser. I was looking for the note that the strange girl had given me, but it was missing!

I turned to ask Nathan if he had seen it, but he was already fast asleep. I flicked off the light and crashed onto the bed for a good night's sleep – but just as I began to fall asleep I heard something smash against our window! I almost jumped out of my skin!

Chapter Seventeen

"Nathan! Nathan, did you hear that?" I whispered fiercely.

"Whaa…what?" asked Nathan.

Then it happened again! Someone was pelting rocks at our window. I jumped out of bed and threw my jeans on.

"Where are you going?" asked Nathan as he was starting to get out of bed, too.

"C'mon! Get dressed. It's obvious that Nancy girl knows something! And I want to find out what it is!" I said.

"But it's dark outside…" grumbled Nathan.

"Yeah…but this just might be the best time to see the lake monster, sea serpent, Champ, or whatever it is! C'mon get dressed…I can't solve this myth alone!" I pleaded.

Nathan just shook his head, sighed and quickly got dressed while I scribbled a note to our parents and taped it to the outside of our cabin door.

We grabbed our Myth Solver backpacks and left. We slid down the sandy bluff while I shined my flashlight toward the bottom where the rocks had come from.

"Over here!" said a girl's voice.

"Who's there?" I whispered.

"It's me, Nancy!" she answered.

"And me, Sissy!"

"What? What the heck is going on here?" I asked as we walked up to them, shining our flashlights.

"Mick...you have got to believe this girl! She has told me the whole story and we have to go check it out!" exclaimed Sissy.

"Oh...so you took the note! I thought you didn't believe in lake monsters!" I said.

"Yeah, I took the note...well, I didn't actually take it, like I found it lying on the floor. But it's a good thing I did! I am surprised at your stubbornness, Mick Morris. I thought you wanted to find Champ!" snapped Sissy.

"Alright, you two...not again. We are here to find Champ and it looks like Nancy is ready to go," Nathan said as he pointed at Nancy, who had now climbed into a small cubby cabin speed boat that was tied up at the dock.

"So, let's go...Hi, I'm Mick, and this is Nathan, and I guess you already know Sissy."

"Hi. Nice to meet you. I'm Nancy."

"I just have one question. How did you get into our cabin?" I asked.

"What?" asked Nancy.

"Oh...uh...that was me," said Sissy, while we all climbed into the boat and put on life vests. "I, uh, well I knew you wouldn't go...So, I just thought I would freak you out about it a bit..."

Chapter Eighteen

What we didn't know was just how freaked out we were going to be within the next few minutes!

We shoved off from shore. Nancy had the running lights on and the front navigation light shined an unnatural streak across the black water.

We couldn't start the motor yet because it would wake everyone in the cabins, so we used oars to row out for a while. Once we were about 100 feet out, Nancy quietly revved up the engine and guided the boat toward the middle of the deep dark lake. It was pitch black outside, except for the moon shining brightly on the lake and the twinkling stars. It was wild at night on the water because we all had a ghostlike blue look to ourselves.

We could see there were no more cabins, just the outline of rugged cliffs and jagged inlets to the side.

Once we were further out into the lake, Nancy cut the engine and we just drifted.

"So, tell us about your Champ findings," I said to Nancy as we all sat in the back of the boat.

"Well...it all started when I was five years old and out fishing with my grandfather..." Nancy began.

But her words were cut short when we heard some loud splashing.

"What was that?" asked Sissy.

Nathan and I shined our flashlights on the water and around the perimeter of the boat, but we could only see the waves flapping in the wind.

"Hey, it's getting cold out here…shouldn't we get the camera ready or something?" asked Sissy as she looked in her backpack for her sweatshirt, "and what is that splashing?"

"You know, that didn't sound like the regular waves…" exclaimed Nancy as she stood up.

She was right! It wasn't the regular waves at all! *In fact, there was nothing regular about it, because seconds later we were attacked by Champ!*

Chapter Nineteen

Suddenly the boat violently shifted to one side!

"Hang on!" screamed Nancy over the low idle of the engine, as we all flew to the other side of the boat. But before we could grab onto anything – the boat violently hurled the other way! *We were being tossed every which way!*

Nancy gunned the engine while telling everyone to hold on! She yanked the steering wheel with all her might as she tried to take the boat in a different direction…but it was no use! Every time she would turn we would be thrown in a different direction. It was almost as if the monster was slapping the boat back and forth!

It seemed to go on forever! Then it suddenly stopped. I looked around the boat and realized Nathan was missing!!!

The boat was slippery with seaweed and water as I slid while trying to hold onto the sides and grip the flashlight while searching for Nathan!

"Nathan!!!" I screamed at the top of my lungs. "Nathan, can you hear me???"

"Don't answer him, Nathan…don't answer him! The creature is somewhere out there! Champ will get him if he answers! Put the flashlight out!!!" screamed Nancy.

She was right. In another few seconds the boat was slammed into, as Sissy screamed at the top of her lungs.

"Quiet…we've got to remain quiet!" yelled Nancy as she cut the engine completely. We all froze and then seconds later we heard an enormous splash. I quietly turned to look overboard. I frantically searched for my best friend. As I looked toward the splash, from the glow of the moon I could see an enormous black slithery dinosaur-looking body with an enormous hump in the shadows. The entire length of it had knife-like edges and an unbelievably long neck and head as it smoothly swam away.

Sissy remained frozen, clinging to the side of the boat. I turned to find Nathan. I was so afraid Champ had gotten him!

"Nathan, Nathan…" I whispered as I scanned the back of the boat.

Suddenly, a hand covered in seaweed came up in front of my face from the water! I jumped a mile!

Chapter Twenty

"Help me…help me up!" said Nathan.

"Dude! Thank goodness you're alright – I was afraid we had lost you!" I cried. Nathan had managed to grab a waterskiing cord on the back of the boat when he got knocked overboard. Nancy and Sissy came running over as we helped Nathan into the boat.

It was freaky how quiet and calm things had become after such a violent encounter.

"Welcome to your first Champ sighting!" said Nancy, breaking the freakish silence. "I know we're exhausted, but we have to get out of this area before it comes back."

"Comes back? Comes back?" cried Sissy.

"Yeah…it has a tendency to do that…every time I've come out near this inlet…this is where I…" But Nancy was interrupted when another huge thump hit the boat.

"See what I mean, we gotta get out of here now!" yelled Nancy as she went to start the engine.

As she turned the key over…there was nothing but a hollow click! The engine was dead! The boat wouldn't start! And we could hear the loud slithering laps in the water coming right back our way!

"Now what?" I hollered.

"Everybody lay down and just hold on as tight as you can…he is coming in again!" screamed Nancy.

"He…how do you know it's a he?" asked Nathan.

"I don't!" yelled Nancy, and just that instant the boat tilted to the side and was lifted upward as we tumbled backwards into the cubby cabin!

We were in a pile on top of each other, scrambling to get our bearings when we could feel the boat rise up above the water!

46

"Oh my gosh! What is happening?" cried Sissy.

"It's lifting up the boat!" whispered Nancy. "Try not to move or make a sound!"

The boat then began to turn sideways as we were smashed together in the small cabin! Then, seconds later, it tilted the other way. It was almost as if the gigantic monster was trying to shake us out of the boat. We kept as quiet as we could. It seemed like forever, but then the monster just dropped the boat and with a huge splash we were back on the water! The boat was bobbing around from side to side in the water. I was holding onto a bar for dear life with one hand and tightly onto my flashlight with the other.

The next instant would be one of the most terrifying moments ever!

Chapter Twenty-One

As I slowly clicked the flashlight on and pointed toward the doorway of the small cabin…an enormous snakelike, dinosaur head with the longest neck I had ever seen came wrapping around the boat and into the cubby cabin!!!

"AAAAGGGGGHHHHHHHH!!!!" We all screamed at the top of our lungs!

Champ's massive head was right in front of us! It had huge rows of shark-like teeth and beady yellow eyes. It instantly reminded me of some sort of T-rex sea serpent…but with a neck so long you could swear it was a snake!

Out of pure instinct I threw the flashlight right at the massive beast and hit him right in the face! It made a weird moaning sound, recoiled, then slithered back under water. We just laid there silent; nobody moved a muscle! A few minutes seemed like hours as the boat rocked and creaked on the waves.

"Is everybody okay?" I finally whispered.

"Uh…think so," replied Nathan.

"Yeah, okay," said Nancy.

"Sissy…are you alright?" I asked as we all began to slowly get up. "Sissy?"

"Well, if you call almost being eaten alive by a giant dinosaur, fish, serpent, snake thingy okay…well, then yes, I guess I'm fine!" said Sissy.

"We have an extra set of oars under the seats on the side," said Nancy.

Nathan dug out his flashlight and very quietly and carefully we began to creep out of the cabin and to the back of the boat.

We followed Nathan's flashlight. It was still dark out, but the moonlight was helping us to see. The water was still and quiet…for now.

Chapter Twenty-Two

"Oh my gosh!" yelled Sissy.

"What?" I asked, fearing for what was next.

"Look how far we are from the mainland!" We all turned to see we had drifted miles from our original spot. The few lights that were on land looked like tiny pin dots.

"Oh gross...I think I'm gonna be sick!" said Nathan.

"Does he get seasick?" asked Sissy.

"No...I don't get seasick...but I think you better have a look at this!" said Nathan as he shined his flashlight in the corner of the boat.

"Oooouuuuu...what is that?" asked Sissy.

"It looks like a piece of Champ," said Nancy.

"It sure does; and it smells like it, too!" I said.

It was a thick black and green piece of mushy, leather-like skin. Almost the same kind of hide as an elephant or rhino, and it was oozing a blackish liquid.

"Look! He must've gotten caught on the blade when the engine was tilted up," Nathan said.

Nathan was right. We had lifted the engine up when we were going to try to fix it. We thought the problem with it not starting was seaweed caught on it. That happened right before the last attack!

"I can't believe we actually have a piece of Champ!" I said!

"Unbelievable! Here, put it in this bucket!" exclaimed Nancy, as she pulled a big white fishing bucket from under a seat.

The smell was awful as we stuck it back under the seat.

"We better get rowing!" I said.

When Nathan shined his flashlight around the boat, I was lucky to spot my flashlight…I didn't think it would work, but when I clicked it on – it did!

"Found the oars!" said Nathan.

We had three oars, which would work out perfect. We would try to paddle the boat toward an inlet while Nancy directed the boat.

Or so we thought. No matter how hard we tried to row, the current was going against us and we kept drifting out farther and farther. If we didn't get the engine started; pretty soon we would get to the edge of the long scary lake!

"Nathan, you hold the flashlight and I'll take a look at the engine!" I said.

Nathan tried to steady the flashlight.

"Nancy, give it a try!" I yelled.

Nancy turned the key again. Nothing but a dead click!

"Okay! I think I see what the problem is…Sissy, please bring me my backpack!" I yelled anxiously.

Sissy quickly felt around the bottom of the boat and started to drag over every backpack she could find. Nathan shined his flashlight over them and I could see mine. I quickly unzipped a pocket and pulled out a case that held an assortment of tools. I pulled out pliers and went back to work on the engine.

"Try now!" I yelled.

Nancy tried the engine again it sounded like it was about to turn over, but for some reason it just wouldn't catch!

Now we were drifting farther and farther away! The waves were getting rougher! If we didn't get that engine fixed and quick, our worst fate would happen in this tiny boat!

Chapter Twenty-Three

"Mick, hold up," said Nathan. "I think I see a loose wire under the spark plug you just tightened!"

Nathan was right. I took the flashlight from him and he quickly went to work on the tiny wire. He was good at that and it reminded him of when he works his genius on computers back home.

"Now try!" yelled Nathan. As Nancy turned the key we all held our breath...the engine turned over! Only this time it didn't sputter out! It revved up!

"Hold on!" she yelled and made a sharp turn as we headed back to shore...but we weren't alone!

As I glanced back over my shoulder I could see a huge black form hot on our trail once again!

We were flying over the choppy lake and Champ was after us! The hideous lake monster was rolling in and out of the water with its snake-like movement. In the shadows of the night I could see its jagged outline and unbelievably long neck as it was gaining on us!

"Nancy...we've got to go faster!" I screamed.

"It's following us!" I yelled.

But for some reason it wasn't attacking us...until we got close to the same area it had attacked us before!

Seconds later, the giant beast with its enormous, horrifying long neck began to wrap itself around the boat. Its giant black flippers with sharp protruding claws seemed to be trying to slap at the boat again!

"Hang on!" I yelled.

The weirdest thing was that every time we got in that same area – near a small inlet – the giant lake monster would show up and freak out…almost as if it wanted it us away from that inlet!

But this time it was hitting the boat so hard, that with one big swoop it launched the boat into the air! We were actually airborne…in a boat!

This is where the story stops. Now it's your turn! That's right. You get to decide which way you would like the story to go. There are *'Five Ways to Finish'* this book and it's up to you to decide.

1) For a normal ending, go to page…………….55.
2) For a very scary ending, go to page………......97.
3) For a freakish fairy tale ending, go to page…132.
4) For a shocking sci-fi ending, go to page……156.
5) For an instant message ending, go to page….194.

Chapter One - Normal

The airborne boat started pointing downward! We were holding on as tight as we could and screaming! Within seconds, the small boat hit the side of a steep cliff, then bounced through a small rock wall opening that lead into a tiny hidden cove. Then as we plunged straight into a sand bar, we all went flying out of the boat into what seemed to be a small lagoon.

The next thing we knew there was an avalanche! The cliff the boat had bounced off of caused rocks to fall! We quickly scrambled out of the lagoon and onto shore. We could see hundreds of rocks falling and splashing into the water. Pebbles were hitting us as the massive cliff completely collapsed!

"Back up!" Nathan screamed at the top of his lungs.

Nathan and I grabbed Sissy and Nancy and pulled them into a huddle while covering our heads! Rocks of all sizes were tumbling down! They were filling the small opening of the tiny cove the boat had come through! They piled up on top of each other, half covering the boat and blocking us from the black waters of Lake Champlain!

When the rocks finally stopped tumbling, it was clear we were completely trapped!

The sky had begun to turn to dawn as the outline of the half-buried boat stuck in a sea of rocks on a sand bar was visible.

The four of us sat there stunned, while coughing as we dusted off the sand and dirt that covered us. We could now see the rugged shoreline that lined the little beach. It circled just behind a small thatch of brush and a few trees. Behind the trees, the cliffs were almost straight up and down. The small entrance to the cove was now completely walled off. When the dust finally cleared we just looked around in awe.

"I've had enough of this!" stated Sissy as she stood up.

"I am so sorry I got you into this mess!" cried Nancy.

"No…not that! I meant I am sick and tired of being wet," wailed Sissy, as she began wading through the tiny pool to the boat.

"Where are you going?" I asked.

"Didn't you hear me? I said I am sick and tired of being soaking wet…I am going to try to get a dry sweatshirt out of my backpack!" Sissy snapped back with her hands on her hips as she began walking into the water. *But that may have been her biggest mistake.*

Chapter Two – Normal

"Sissy, stop! Those rocks could begin falling again!" I screamed as I got up and went to follow her to the boat. Then, just as I was about two inches from the water...

"Wha...wha...what was that?" Sissy asked, sounding frightened as she stopped walking.

"What? What was what?" I asked.

"I felt something weird swimming around my legs..." Sissy exclaimed, now waist deep in water, "Oooouuu! That felt big and slimy."

"It's probably just a fish," said Nathan.

The sun was starting to come up now and we all began to wade into the murky water toward Sissy. We were completely startled when Sissy screamed, "It's wrapping around my legs!"

"Maybe it's a water snake!" yelled Nancy.

Seconds later, we could feel long snake-like things and flippers hitting our legs.

"Quick, everyone out of the water!" I yelled as we ran back to shore.

"Are snakes, like, common in these parts?" Nathan asked Nancy, who was shaking.

She shook her head no, while staring at the water. It was now perfectly still.

"Maybe it was just seaweed," I said.

But Sissy insisted it was some kind of long, slimy living creature. We waited awhile, sitting on the beach staring at the calm water…the sun was now shining and we were relieved it was daylight.

We knew our only hope was to find a way to dig out the boat…and we were going have to wade through the spooky water to get to it. *But the question was, what if there really was something in that water – something that would get us first?*

Chapter Three - Normal

"Alright…we can't just sit here all day. We have to get to that boat to see if that radio is still working. And we have to get our backpacks. I'll go in," I said, trying as hard as I could to hide my fear.

Nathan nodded in agreement while getting up to join me. We made Sissy and Nancy wait on the shore. We moved slowly and carefully through the dark water to the boat, unsure about what was lurking just below the surface.

Within seconds, I could feel the slimy, snake-like creature! I tried to ignore it and continued walking!

I glanced over at Nathan and he had that 'I'm so grossed out' kind of look on his face. I knew instantly he was feeling the slithery things, too.

We continued moving steadily toward the boat while something kept swimming by us, brushing up against our legs. It was the weirdest, slimiest sensation.

Before we knew it, a head poked out of the water!!! *It was a long half-horse, half-snake like head!* I freaked, watching in terror as an unbelievably long grey-green colored neck followed! The neck alone had to be at least four feet long. The monster had beady yellow eyes and a double row of shark-like teeth!

I tried to speak, but the words just wouldn't come out of my mouth…

We were frozen with fear as we stared at the miniature creature! I realized it was a baby Champ! Only it wasn't alone! Slowly, one after another poked their pre-historic-looking heads with enormously long necks up out of the water! Until there were four baby Champs just staring at Nathan and me!

"Get out of there right now!" screamed Nancy at the top of her lungs.

But Nathan looked at me as I slowly shook my head 'No.'

Something told me we were okay for the moment. But any sudden movement might startle them into having us for breakfast! I could clearly see their rows of tiny ultra-sharp teeth as the four heads rotated back and forth watching us!

It felt like we were standing there forever, until suddenly one of the big, but baby Champs began to circle around us! It moved with stealth-like speed in the water, doing circles around each of us. Before I knew it, it was right up next to me! I was getting ready to run until it put its face directly next to mine! The lake monster and I were eye to eye! Before I could even blink, it spit a long stream of water right in my face!

Then another one close to Nathan went right up to his face! As Nathan's eyes widened with fear, it did the exact same thing to him! The others joined in as the baby lake monsters kept doing it…over and over.

They were soaking us as they continued to spray water! We couldn't help but burst out laughing! It was almost as if they wanted to play! It was the strangest thing that has ever happened to me in my life! But playing was the last thing on our minds; even though, for the moment, we were just glad they weren't attacking us!

"Dude, let's try to get to the boat," I said as calmly and quietly as I could.

Nathan nodded as we began to move very cautiously toward the boat while being sprayed by the monsters.

Once we got to the side of the boat we could see that a couple of our backpacks were within reach. I slowly leaned into the boat to grab one, when a little Champ locked its razor sharp teeth into my shirt and began tearing at my clothes!

"Oh okay...oooohhhh-k...there you go...uh, little lake monster...baby Champ, sea whatever kind of thingy you are..." I said, frightened, while I gently tried to push it away.

But the more I tried to push it away, the more it tugged on me! Now I was really getting scared!

"I got our backpacks, Mick," said Nathan, as he reached into the boat from the shallow water and grabbed them. Then one of the creatures began to bump into Nathan trying to knock him over! I started splashing water to distract them while Nathan got to shore.

Now I had to get out of there, but when I tried to make my way out of the water, they wouldn't leave me alone! They circled around me! One kept bumping into me with its snout, until it knocked me over! I began falling on top of another one! So I quickly grabbed onto one of its massive fins to catch my balance. As I held onto its fin, it took off swimming!!!

I held on tightly as I climbed on top of the slimy monster. The next thing I knew it was swimming around in circles in the tiny cove…with me riding on its back! I couldn't help but laugh! It was unreal! It was like riding a dolphin in Florida!

Nathan, Sissy, and Nancy couldn't believe their eyes!

Nathan scrambled to get a camera out of the backpack and began snapping pictures…while Sissy and Nancy stood there amazed!

We were all in total disbelief. They could tell I was having so much fun that they decided to run in and give it a try. Each one of them hopped onto a baby Champ! And the weirdest thing was that the baby Champs let them! We were all actually riding around the small lagoon on lake monsters! It was a riot!

It was so much fun that for a few minutes we completely forgot about the horrible situation that we were in…until we were reminded by a loud, weird, horrible moaning sound!!!

Chapter Five - Normal

The instant the moan sounded, the baby Champs completely stopped and violently shook us off their backs. We all went flying into the water!

Afraid of their sudden change, we got back to shore as quickly as we could. The baby Champs went back under water and then resurfaced where the rocks had fallen. It looked like they were trying to get through the wall. They would bump into the rocks, and when they couldn't get through, they would try another spot, and bump into it again. When they realized they couldn't get through they huddled together near the far side of the rocks and floated still and silently.

"That was Champ," said Nancy. "Now I know why she attacked..."

"And, yes...now we know it's a she!" said Sissy, sarcastically staring at Nathan and me.

I just glared at her as Nancy continued...

"Every time I have ever seen Champ it has always been near this cove. Remember last night, whenever we got near this area in the boat she would attack!?"

"That's right!" said Nathan excitedly, "she was trying to protect her young!"

65

"And she, yes, SHE," I said loudly at Sissy, "was trying to hit the boat the other way! But accidentally hit us straight into the cove she was trying to get us away from!

"Exactly!" said Nathan.

"But now we need to find a way out of here…before she finds a way back in!" I exclaimed.

We waded back to the boat and realized if we took the chance of moving the rocks it could cause a deadly avalanche and bury us all. Except there was no other way! We couldn't climb the steep cliffs…and even if we could, Champ's babies wouldn't survive in the cove alone for much longer!

Finally, I had an idea!

Chapter Six - Normal

Back on shore I dug through my Myth Solver backpack until I came across just what I needed…two bungee cords!

"I got them!" I said excitedly, holding them up.

"Oh great, bungee cords, and just how do you propose we get out of this cove while saving these creatures with those?" asked Sissy. "What are we gonna do -- slingshot ourselves out of here?"

"Pretty much!" I grinned, "but not us."

I continued digging and found another cord in my backpack.

"Nathan, do you have any?" I asked.

"You know, I just might!" he smiled, while he began to look through his backpack.

"I'm hot and hungry!" whined Sissy.

"Okay, Nancy, do you have a blanket on that boat?" I asked.

"Yes, but I think it's in the compartment that's buried under rocks."

"Okay," I replied, "no problemo."

"Si…¿Usted es muy feliz ahora?" questioned Nathan in Spanish. Sometimes when things were getting really exciting Nathan would just blurt things out in Spanish and I

67

couldn't help but crack up! He would forget that I didn't understand him.

"Si, quesadilla," I responded.

I didn't know if what I just said was that funny, or the total fear and tenseness we were all feeling, but we all burst out laughing…until we heard the groaning sounds and knew if we didn't work fast, this situation was going to be anything but funny!

We focused on my plan. Sissy was the lightest, so she climbed into the boat. Very carefully we began to remove some of the rocks off the seats. It was the back of the boat that was half buried but we still didn't want to rock the boat. Once we were able to open the compartment, we were thrilled to find two blankets. There was also rope and some other supplies we could use…but we couldn't believe what we found next!

In the very bottom of the seat compartment, hidden under the other supplies, was an old brown cardboard box. Sissy tried to lift it out but it was too heavy, so I had to carefully climb into the boat to help. It was a dangerous operation while we tried to be as gentle as possible lifting out the heavy box without moving the boat! It took two of us to lift it out. It was so old that the cardboard was rotting. It had a faded label and written on it was:

To Nancy, Champ scouting supplies...because you just never know! Love, your grandfather.

"I can't believe it! He was the only one who knew Champ existed! He always believed me when I told him I had seen Champ. He gave me this boat!" Nancy exclaimed as tears welled up in her eyes. "He always said, 'you just never know!'"

But, apparently, Nancy's grandfather did know! He knew enough to pack supplies in case of an emergency...and these were the best supplies we could have ever hoped for! We quickly opened up the box and couldn't believe our eyes!

"A dinghy!!!" I shouted out at the top of my lungs.

"Yeah!" everybody screamed.

"Yeah! Yeah! Yeah!" Sissy screamed as she clapped her hands repeatedly, until we were all looking at her as she stopped and asked, "but what the heck's a dinghy?"

"It's an inflatable boat!" I exclaimed.

"Okaaaaayyy, so why so excited? We have a real boat!" she snickered.

"Yeah, well, you just go see if you can get the boat out from under those rocks!" I snapped.

"And look!" yelled Nathan as we lifted out the compact dinghy, not paying attention to what Sissy was up to. In the bottom of the box was a pump!

But seconds later, it was too late. The boat's engine revved up as Sissy stood at the wheel...*and the rocks began to fall!*

Chapter Eight – Normal

"What are you doing?" I screamed at the top of my lungs! "Get out of there! Right NOOOOOWWW!!!"

Nathan and Nancy grabbed the supplies while I grabbed Sissy and pulled her overboard, just missing a shower of rocks! I was pulling her along, while running as fast as we could back to the shore.

Once on land, we backed up into the small bushes, trees and sea grass, as far against the cliff as we could to avoid the avalanche of rocks!

Luckily, it didn't last too long.

"Just what were you trying to do?" I snapped.

"I thought you were serious, Mick, when you told me to just see if I could get the boat out from under the rocks!" Sissy explained.

"No, Sissy, I was not serious. I was just kidding," I barked while trying to hold back my anger. This was the first trip she had really pushed my buttons.

"Okay, then I'm sorry, alright? Forgive me? You have to, you are related to me…you're my cuz, remember cousins?" she teased.

'Cousins, yeah, lucky me,' I thought to myself. That was something that at this moment I would like to forget!

When the last pebbles stopped tumbling, we crawled out to the beach. The baby Champs were still huddled safely in the far corner.

"Mick, I have a feeling they need their mother," said Nancy.

"Yeah, I do too," I replied, not realizing just how soon they would be with her!

Nathan began to fill the dinghy with air, while Sissy and Nancy doubled the blankets and attached a bungee cord hook through each corner. We were lucky enough that Nathan had found two bungee cords in his backpack.

We knew the only way we were going to get out of the rock sealed cove would be to get our trapped boat out. But we would have to move the little Champs out first. Because even if we could get out of the cove, if we left them behind, Champ would make sure to get us! Champ was smart enough to know we were in there with her young!

Seconds later, we wouldn't have time to think about whether or not our plan would work...

"Ahhhhhoooouuuunnn!!!" There it was again! That ghastly, shocking, growling-like groan filled the air! It sounded like a T-rex sound effect from the movies! Only this time it seemed like it was just above us. *As I looked up toward the top of the rocks, my heart stopped beating! I was horrified when I saw what I saw!*

Chapter Nine – Normal

There was Champ! The lake monster had finally managed to scale up the other side of the rocks! It was now at the top looking down!

It was clear the monster was filled with rage…its ferocious mouth wide open as its dangerous teeth glistened in the sunlight. It swung its gigantic head wildly back and forth!

It didn't see us at first. We quickly backed up and hid in the brush next to the cliff walls.

"Oh, no…now what?" whispered Sissy.

Champ was eyeing the lagoon…but when she saw her young, she opened her mouth wide open and let out another ear deafening moan. Then she did the unthinkable!

Champ began to try to come down into the lagoon! But every time she would put one of her giant flipper fins down, rocks would plummet below!

"Just keep calm, whatever you do…" I whispered.

It was apparent that if Champ moved one more inch the rocks would crash down and kill us all!

"Nathan, why aren't her young hearing her?" I asked.

"I don't know. Maybe they have gotten too weak, being without her all this time," Nathan replied.

He was right. The hot sun was beating down as it was getting later in the day. But now what? What if Champ thought we had hurt her babies?

"Are you thinking what I'm thinking?' I asked.

"Yeah, that she's gonna come looking for us first!" answered Nathan.

It was like we were in a stalemate. Like in chess, nobody could make a move without losing. Before I knew it, Sissy had pulled out her fearless self and began moving ever so slowly through the small bushes and sea grass toward the end of the rock wall. I couldn't yell at her to stop, it would startle Champ. The next thing I knew she was carefully slipping into the water.

Within seconds, Champ saw Sissy! Sissy froze when Champ bellowed again. Champ then leaned her unbelievably long neck down toward the lagoon!

Sissy didn't move.

I couldn't hold back any longer, "Sissy come back here!" I yelled.

Champ began growling wildly as Sissy slowly continued.

"No! Somebody's got to show her that her babies are alright…or we will all be here staring at each other until either those rocks fall or Champ decides to take a chance!

"Once I show her the babies are all okay…you guys will have to move quick with the slingshot!"

This was one time I couldn't argue with Sissy. *This would be our only chance to rescue ourselves, and them!*

Chapter Ten - Normal

Sissy continued moving very slowly; this time Champ's beady yellow eyes followed her every move, while snarling and making dreadful growling sounds. It was obvious the ferocious lake monster was ready to strike at any second!

All we could hope for was that those babies were alright. Because if they weren't, we were finished! Champ would think we hurt them and would destroy us!

Nathan and I helped Nancy fold the blankets so we could open them easily and quickly to launch one of the babies!

Sissy was still moving very slowly toward the huddled group, while the enormous angry Champ looked on.

We knew we couldn't startle Champ. As Sissy inched her way over, keeping Champ's attention, we carefully moved out of bushes and trees, so we would be ready to move.

The closer Sissy got, the more violently Champ howled and waved her head!

"Careful, Sissy." I whispered.

She was almost there now, almost to the huddle. Then Sissy instinctively put her hands over her head, almost to let Champ know she meant no harm. Champ was so engrossed in what Sissy was doing we were able to move out into view…or so we thought!

Chapter Eleven – Normal

Once again, Champ began to stretch her long neck from where she stood at the top of the rocks into the lagoon. We froze in our tracks. Her wicked jaws were grinding back and forth…the two rows of huge sharp teeth grinding, ready to attack!

"Don't move!" said Nathan.

"Sissy, move those babies…and fast!" I yelled.

Rocks were beginning to plummet from the top, but luckily, Champ's neck was too short to reach all the way down!

Sissy slowly lowered her arms into the water and tried to wake one of the babies. It was odd that it was a baby but still five times bigger than Sissy. She continued to keep her eye on Champ while gently petting the baby.

Champ was starting to get restless and was clearly looking for other ways to get to us!

But something was wrong! The baby wouldn't wake up!!!

"Sissy, pet them harder," I yelled.

"No!" said Nancy, "I've read about this, they are pre-historic. If you startle them they could hurt you, Sissy. They have got to see you! You are going to have to go under water and try to get their attention!"

Immediately, Sissy went under water, she put her hands back up…which was a relief for me to be able to see that she was moving around and alright.

Seconds later, she was back up but the babies still hadn't moved!

"Now what? I got right in front of their face and I even opened my eyes in this gross water!" stated Sissy impatiently.

"They are a lot like snakes, Sissy…even though some people think they are a species of the plesiosaurus…but just like reptiles, most of them can't see directly in front of them. Back up a couple of inches," said Nancy.

We were trying to keep our composure as we watched Sissy go under again…but this time she didn't keep her hands up. It seemed like minutes had gone by and Sissy hadn't come up for air! I began to feel sick to my stomach!

Chapter Twelve – Normal

I dropped my corner of the slingshot, but the minute I did, Champ wailed and kicked rocks our way with her giant flipper. She was warning me I better stay put. I didn't know what to do!

It seemed like a long time had gone by and Sissy was still under water. Just as I was about to jump in and take the chance of Champ coming after us all – Sissy poked her head out of the water and immediately following her was a baby Champ!

"Ahhhhhooooouuuunnn!" Champ bellowed again.

Now we had to move and fast, before this enormous lake monster got any more irritated!

We didn't have to make our way too far into the water…the baby was already trying to swim to its mother! But we had to stop it from trying to climb up the rocks!

We quickly circled around it as Nathan and I guided the baby onto the dinghy, then slid it onto the slingshot. Sissy and Nancy pulled the blankets underneath it, so it was now in the middle of the blankets. While Nathan and I went under the blanket holding tightly, Sissy and Nancy pulled the other sides as far as they could while keeping the baby secured with a bungee cord across the front of him.

Champ swung her enormous head around while watching our far-fetched scheme. But if it worked, it would mean we were free to escape without having to worry about being attacked. They pulled back farther, when the bungee cords were as taunt as they could possibly be, we all got ready…

"On the count of three…" I said.

"One, two, three!" we said in unison and quickly released the cord that held the baby Champ, and sent it flying up over the rocks and past its mother. Immediately, Champ dove down onto the other side of Lake Champlain!

Chapter Thirteen - Normal

We worked quickly, knowing we had only minutes before Champ would be back looking for the others. Now the baby Champs were starting to wake up and move around; which meant they were a lot harder to round up and place in the slingshot!

We finally corralled another and just in time, we could see by the pebbles falling that Champ was on her way back up the other side. We loaded the slimy baby into the slingshot. Once again, on the count of three, we gently pulled and pulled, all the way back, then released! It went soaring over the rock wall, just as we could see Champ's huge head beginning to show over the wall. Again, she followed her baby to the other side.

The third one was even harder to catch, and a lot less willing to be strapped down. We were really struggling with it, but we finally managed to strap it in and sent it flying.

"We're almost there, dude!" yelled Nathan excitedly, as we continued to try to catch the last baby.

"I think you spoke too soon," said Sissy. This time, the last baby was no longer in a sleepy daze. It was wide awake and moving around the small body of water with amazing speed. It started to spit again as it slipped between us. It seemed to think that once again this was a game!

"You two, go that way!" I yelled to Nathan and Nancy, "while Sissy and I close in over here!"

But it was hopeless. The baby continued to dodge us – no matter what we tried. We had run out of time! Champ was climbing up the fragile rocks to get the last of her young...and we knew we had better deliver!

Chapter Fourteen – Normal

Almost instantly, the baby Champ slowed down and stopped playing. We managed to corner it!

"I got him!" I screamed as I grabbed onto one of its fins, but it began to struggle away from me!

"Nathan, help me! I can't hold onto it!" I yelled as Nathan came over, helping me wrestle the monster into our homemade slingshot. By now it was even harder to use. The blankets were soaked!

This time it seemed like it was going to be impossible and time was running out! If Champ saw us wrestling with her last baby, she would be furious! Who knows what she would do!

"I have an idea! Why don't you try to ride it again," exclaimed Nancy, "then you can circle it back to right in front of the slingshot!"

It seemed like a silly idea, but it was worth a chance. I still had a hold of its flipper as I threw myself onto it. Within seconds, the thing was happily swimming around in circles.

"Okay, that a boy, good little lake monster!" I exclaimed as I petted its long neck, "When I get close…get ready!"

They pulled back the slingshot. This time I wouldn't be there to help, but if it worked, we would no longer be Champ's target!

I was coming by them, closer, closer...I was getting ready to jump off.

"Now!" I yelled at the top of my lungs, as I jumped off and Nathan wrapped the bungee cord around the lake monster. The instant he did, it began wailing an awful, loud sound.

Immediately following the baby's cry came the horrible, frightening moan of Champ coming back up over the rocks! But this time, she wasn't alone!

Chapter Fifteen – Normal

I shuddered when Champ poked her head up over the top of the rocks again…but that was nothing compared to what came next! Another enormous lake monster head came right up next to her! It looked like Champ, only it was twice the size of Champ's! It had a huge head – but it was darker in color and had twice as many rows of razor-sharp teeth!

"Looks like…mo…mo…mommy brought the…the d…daddy this time" Sissy stuttered with fear.

"No kidding" said Nathan breathlessly, while we both let go of their baby the instant that it began howling and swimming toward its parents.

The two humongous Champs were now at the rock wall…flailing their heads around madly, while growling and sneering. By now, the baby had gotten to the bottom of the rocks! There was nothing we could do but stand and watch as the enormous mother Champ begin to try to make her way down the loose crumbling rocks…As they began to fall, she let out such an ear-deafening wail that we had to cover our ears!

Sissy and Nancy quickly began to make their way over to the baby who was getting pelted with rocks!

"Stop!" I screamed at them.

"It's no use, Mick…if that baby dies, then we all do!" cried Sissy.

She was right!

"Okay, but move very slowly…" I whispered as we went to help.

The Champs were watching our every move. The baby had calmed down now as we gently pulled it back across the tiny lagoon with us. It was as if things were suspended in time, like everything was in slow motion. The only thing going fast was my heart; it was beating so hard it was about to pop out of my chest!

Once we were back on the other side of the lagoon, both the mother and the father Champ disappeared down other side of the wall.

"What are they doing?" asked Nancy.

"If my calculations serve me right, I would say they are removing the formations one by one to cause an inverted…" Nathan continued.

"English, Nathan, English!" I said.

"But I wasn't even speaking Spanish. Oh, okay! Well, they are removing the rocks from the other side, so the wall levels out and they can get in here to get little Champ," replied Nathan.

Every one of us looked at each other as our eyes widened! If they came into the lagoon, what would that mean for us? We were just about to find out!

Chapter Sixteen - Normal

Within seconds, they had dug out so many rocks, the wall was now almost completely gone! The boat began to float freely. They were now coming straight at us! These huge prehistoric, serpent, dinosaur-like monsters howling at the top of their lungs! Once they had scaled the wall, the rocks melted into the water and the entire cove was filled with waves from their humongous size! The closer they came the more we backed up.

"Mick, what now?" cried Sissy.

"I think we should send this one in the direction of his parents!" I yelled.

We were in such shock at these gigantic beasts that were coming our way, we hadn't even thought to let go of the young one! But it was something we wouldn't have to worry about. It shook itself loose and swam directly toward its mother! But big daddy Champ continued looming toward us! By now we had backed up onto the tiny shoreline and were totally pressed against the rocky cliff!

He was waving his ferocious head back and forth and growling wildly! He was just a few feet away from us…we knew we were doomed! Suddenly, a huge screech came from behind him! He stopped dead in his tracks and tossed his mammoth head to look back…It's giant clawed, flipper foot was right in front of us. It lifted up on its tiny back legs, as if it was going to swat us. But then plopped it in the water facing the other way as it slowly turned around!

The mother Champ had actually yelled at him! She must've told him to leave us alone, because he was now heading back to her and the baby. His huge, long, dark tail flipping behind him as it leveled everything it struck!

The baby climbed on his back and in seconds they were over what was left of the wall. On the other side, the three other babies glided over to them and slid onto their backs.

The sun was shining so brightly and bouncing off the waves, we could hardly see their massive humps and babies as they were rolling up and down into the water. They were so smooth that they could've been easily mistaken for giant logs drifting on the shiny lake surface…until they gently disappeared under the water.

Chapter Seventeen – Normal

We heard sobbing sounds behind us and turned to see Nancy crying. When Sissy saw her, she started to cry, too.

"What's wrong…we're okay, we're alive! They're gone!" I said, completely relieved.

"It was just so…so…" began Sissy until I interrupted, "Frightening? I know. Man, that was close, wasn't it?"

"Not that…you dork…it was, well, touching," she cried.

"Touching? Touching?! I'll say it was touching! We were almost eaten! How's that for touching?" I exclaimed.

"Girls are just crazy," said Nathan, shaking his head and stunned, while I made a totally disgusted face at them and said, "And don't get all choked up just yet, because we aren't quite out of here!"

"The boat!" yelled Nathan.

We all turned to see the boat was now slowly drifting out of the opening in the tiny lagoon and into the lake!

I began to swim toward it! Nathan followed, while Nancy and Sissy grabbed our Myth Solver backpacks off the shore. I got to the boat first. I managed to grab on and climb in. The anchor was still covered with rocks as I dug it out as fast as I could, threw it overboard and jumped back into the water to help the others climb in.

"What is that awful, awful smell?" asked Sissy.

"I bet I know," answered Nathan, as he went and opened up the other seat compartment and we all gagged as we were overwhelmed with the terrible odor.

"Uh...I think we can throw that out now, unless anyone wants it for a souvenir," I said as I covered my nose and picked up the smelly white bucket and dumped the small souvenir piece of Champ overboard.

We finished emptying the rocks out of the boat and tried to start the engine.

It sputtered, then slowly turned over! We all took one last look at the tiny cove and realized the little yellow dinghy was still on the shore.

"I'll leave it there for next time," said Nancy as she took the steering wheel, gunned the engine and began to steer us out into the lake. She made sure we were far out enough away from inlets, while going slowly. We wanted to make sure we weren't going to ride over any Champs or disturb any of their nests ever, ever again!

When we got near the shore, we could see there were tons of people on the bluff near the cabins.

"What's going on?" I asked as I dug my binoculars out of my backpack.

"Maybe they're worried about us," said Sissy.

"But I left a note right on our door!" I exclaimed.

As we got closer I could see many of the people were pointing and the crew had their cameras out and were filming.

We docked at the pier near the cabins and quickly climbed up the bluff. I made my way through the crowd of people to the set. It was strange, nobody even noticed us as they just stared at the lake.

The crew was busy; lights were set up and cameras were filming while Mom and Dad were doing a voiceover on the set...

"I have to say, in my opinion, that is not a log, or a sturgeon, or any other fish that is common for this region," Dad said excitedly.

"I have to agree with you. It's nothing like we have ever seen! What an exciting day for Uncover! Well, thanks for joining us on our most successful mission to Lake Champlain...and you decide -- was it reality or just a myth?" added Mom.

The familiar Uncover show music came up. It was usually dropped in during the studio edits, unless there was a crowd of people and something exciting was happening, and this was exciting!

"That's a wrap!" yelled Mr. Juarez, Nathan's dad.

Mom took her microphone off and came running over to me...

"Hi, my son! Did you see it? Mick, did you see Champ? It had to be him!" exclaimed Mom.

"I'm sure it was something, we didn't even have time to get on the boats...and there it was. And not just one, but a whole herd of them swam by!" exclaimed Dad as he joined us.

"A family…you mean a family," said Sissy happily, until she realized what she had done. Everyone was looking at her as she stopped and slowly covered her own mouth with her hand.

Chapter Nineteen - Normal

"What? What did…" Aunt Marisa asked as she walked up.

"She's joking! You know, my cuz…sometimes it's just hard to take her seriously," I said.

"Mick, you don't even seem excited!" said Mom.

"And just wait 'til you see the footage!" said Dad.

"Hey, where have you been anyway? And what happened to your clothes? Look at all of you…what happened?" asked Mom.

"Uhhh…we were, uh, just doing s-s-some…" stuttered Nathan.

"Snorkeling!" chirped Sissy.

"Really? Where…in the sand?" Mom laughed, and quickly got pulled away by the script supervisor.

That was lucky, I thought to myself!

As I glanced toward the crew, Dennis Hinkelson caught my eye – he was just standing there watching us, shaking his head…

The sighting at Lake Champlain was over and the crowd began to break up, except around Nancy. She had her own crowd. We turned to see her in the middle of the same group of kids who had made fun of her. She was just shrugging her shoulders; then she pushed her way out to join us.

"They believe you now, don't they?" I asked.

"You know it's kind of funny, I don't really care what they think or what they do or don't believe," replied Nancy. "And I will never tell anyone what happened to us."

"Mmmmm, mmmm," sighed Nathan.

"Nope! Me neither," I replied smiling.

"But what about the photos?" asked Sissy.

"I'll give them to my grandkids. With a dinghy..." answered Nancy. We all laughed and headed to the big barn as the Pine Lake Resort dinner bell rang.

The End

Chapter One - Scary

It was as if time had slowed down. We were sailing through the air in slow motion. It was all we could do to hold on! Everyone was screaming as the boat slowly began tilting downward…we were going to crash!

The tip of the boat hit the water with such force that it bounced back up into the air. Then it plopped down, while rocking from side-to-side. We were too shook up to move!

"Hey…Nathan, Sissy, Nancy…anyone?" I whispered while I held on as tight as I could to the side of the boat.

"Yeah…over here!" said Nathan. I slowly released my hand and crawled over to him while trying to keep my balance.

"Man…I bumped my head…I can feel a huge goose egg!" Nathan said, rubbing his head.

"Ohhhhhh…ohhhhhhh…am I alive or am I dead?" moaned Sissy.

"You're alive…you okay?" I asked as I slowly began to feel my way around the boat to find Sissy.

"Hey! Watch where you put your hands!" barked Sissy.

"Oops…I'm sorry. Now I know by your tone of voice that you're fine!" I said as I tried to find a flashlight, knowing in my heart they had to have gone flying out of the boat when it crashed down.

"Whew…I'm over here," whispered Nancy, "but I really think we should try to remain quiet for a bit…just to make sure Champ doesn't hear us."

But it was too late! The lapping sounds began to grow louder as it headed our way again…Champ was back after us!

Chapter Two - Scary

"Start the engine!" I screamed at the top of my lungs. Nancy frantically began to make her way to the driver's seat.

"Find the oars…maybe we can beat it off!" hollered Nathan as we scrambled to find them, but the splashes were getting louder!

"The key! It's gone!" screamed Nancy. "It must've fallen out!" It was total chaos until we found the oars. Seconds later, the enormous beast lifted its massive long neck and head above the boat!

Its razor-sharp teeth were glowing as it opened its mouth, ready to take a bite out of us, or the boat…whichever its horrible mouth struck first!

Almost instantly, it was much easier to see the repulsive monster as a glimpse of the sun popped above the lake.

But as fast as the beast had risen out of the water it sunk back down!

"Wha…what happened?" asked Sissy, her voice trembling.

"I don't know" I replied breathlessly.

We slowly crawled over to the edge of the boat, but there was no sign of Champ! We looked everywhere. It was now easy to see, since daylight was breaking, but there was nothing, just a lone seagull floating on the waves!

"Where'd he go?" asked Nathan.

"I don't know…and I don't really want to find out!" I said.

We searched for the key but it was gone. We could see that to get back to Port Henry from where we were with just a couple of oars would take us forever. We pulled out our new walkie-talkies and flipped a switch. But we decided that if we used them we would only get in trouble for being so far away from the cabins. Our parents and the crew probably wouldn't believe what happened anyway. We decided our best bet would be to get to the nearest shore.

With a little help from the waves we finally reached land. We pulled the boat up on a gravelly beach and walked into town. We were now in Vermont!

Chapter Three - Scary

We walked down the lonely street. There wasn't a soul in sight. We were exhausted and hungry.

"There, look!" said Nancy, pointing at a tiny corner diner with an 'open' sign in the window.

We went in to the small restaurant. It had three booths with red vinyl seats that lined the windows. Across from them was a counter with the old-fashioned kind of swivel chairs. The walls were lined with stainless steel; the smell of coffee and bacon filled the air. On the counter was a cake holder filled with glazed donuts – it was all we could do to not attack it! We quickly grabbed the nearest booth and looked at the menus.

A waitress in a pale pink uniform walked up, smiling.

"Where you kids from?" she asked.

"Oh, we're with the Myth Solv...ouch! Somebody just kick...*ouch!*" cried Sissy as she looked under the table.

"We are staying with our parents down the road." I interrupted after kicking Sissy.

"WHY DID YOU..." Sissy snapped.

"Ohhh, Sissy...my cousin just loves to joke!" I shouted over Sissy, as I clenched my teeth at her, then turned to the waitress and smiled, "I'll have a sausage, egg and cheese omelet, please."

The waitress looked at me strangely as she finished taking our orders.

"What was that all about? You gave me a bruise, you idiot!" whined Sissy when the waitress left.

"Idiot? Me? Uh…hello…Oh, hi, it's 6:00 in the morning and we are here without our parents. And oh yeah, did I mention that we are staying a gazillion miles from here…and, that's right, we are the Myth Solvers – but without our parents…who are supposed to be the REAL MYTH SOLVERS!" I growled.

"OKAY! I get it!" snarled Sissy.

The waitress walked back up with juice, still looking at us strangely. A few minutes later she brought our food and we ate like we had never eaten before. In between bites, we discussed what happened to the lake monster. Whatever it was, we knew we were lucky…or were we?

Chapter Four - Scary

When we finished, we paid our bill with soggy money and quickly left the diner. We made sure to leave a good tip; we didn't want her to think too much about who we were or what we were doing.

"Get outta here, you gross bird!" yelled Nathan as he shooed away a seagull that had pooped on his shirt. "Yuck!"

"Here's a tissue," said Sissy, pulling one out of her backpack.

We decided the best thing to do would be to get back to Port Henry. Nancy would get her family to come back and help her with the boat later.

We walked to the outer edges of town and sat down on a bench, wondering how we were going to get back to Port Henry.

"Uh, oh, don't look now, Mick, but I think we're in trouble," said Nathan as he pointed to a sheriff's car pulling up.

"Alice tells me you're with the Myth Solver gang that's filming in Port Henry. That true?"

We sat silently for a second until I spoke up. If there was one thing we didn't want to mess around with, it was the law.

"Yes, sir. We are, sir." I answered.

"A bit far from Port Henry, aren't you kids?" he asked.

"Well, you see, officer, my boat broke down," said Nancy as she began to cry.

"No problem. You kids aren't in any trouble. Hop in and I'll take you back to Port Henry," he said.

"Awesome!" I yelled, as Sissy clapped her hands and Nathan yelled, "Yes!"

We piled into the car, Sissy, Nathan and I in the back and Nancy in the front.

The car followed the two-lane highway as we chatted about the Myth Solver show. The sheriff was a big fan and he couldn't wait to meet Mom, Dad and the crew. He told us about Champ sightings. I shivered at the thought.

We passed by a lot of state parks and went over a covered bridge that divided Vermont and New York. We drove past the Adirondack Park Preserve. When we were getting close to Port Henry, we suddenly we came to a strange blackish-green detour sign in the middle of Route 17.

The sheriff stopped the car and immediately got on his car radio to find out about the odd-looking sign. He began telling someone he knew nothing about the sign as he slowly drove down the dirt road detour.

The voice on the radio came back saying there couldn't possibly be a sign there.

"But, Sullivan, I am telling ya...there was this weird detour sign; never saw one like it before, and the road was closed. Now we're headed west down...down... I don't know, I'm not really familiar with this road," he said insistently. After discussing the strange sign, he hung up the radio, shrugged his shoulders and continued down the mysterious twisting dirt road. *Not knowing what horror was waiting just around the bend!*

Chapter Five - Scary

The sky had grown cloudy and dark as the sheriff stopped the car with a jerk.

"I don't know about this detour. It's not going the right way," he stated.

He reached for his car radio again, but this time all he got was static. He slowly pulled the car over to the side of the chilling road.

"You kids wait here...I'm going to see if I can get reception on my cell phone. Lock the doors," he said.

We waited patiently as he dialed. It looked as though he was moving around toward the back of the car to hear. He stopped and tried dialing again, when a seagull dove at him and he shooed it away. He moved further toward the woods. Before we knew it, he was out of sight!

"Where'd he go?" asked Sissy.

"I don't know," I replied.

"Maybe he's just trying to get phone reception," said Nathan.

Seconds later, the sheriff appeared, standing sideways in front of the car. Something was very strange. He looked like he had the cell phone in his hand but that he didn't know what to do with it, so he just threw it. Then he walked over to the car.

"Oooooppeeen uuppp da dooeeerrr!" he said, glaring at us.

As Nancy went to reach for the lock I screamed, "Noooo! Don't touch it!"

"Why?" she asked.

"How come he can't unlock the door himself?" I asked.

"He looks different," said Sissy.

As the sheriff turned to press his face on the window, his eyes looked yellow! The angrier he got, the more his face started to change! It looked horrible, as if his skin was beginning to droop! Almost as if his face was coming off! Underneath was this awful greenish-black scaly skin!

"Agggghhhh!" screamed Sissy.

He had a half-slimy face – but he resembled the sheriff…his face was changing to reveal Champ!!!

Chapter Six - Scary

We were screaming and scared to death! The blood-curdling monster started to jump on the car!

"What's happening!?" screamed Sissy at the top of her lungs. Champ began to wrap his long neck around the entire top of the sheriff's car while staring through the windows!

"He's a shapeshifter!" I screamed.

"A what?" yelled Sissy.

But there wasn't any time to answer. His long tail had now shattered the windshield!

"We have to get out of here…before he gets in!" I hollered.

"Are you crazy?" cried Sissy.

"Mick is right!" said Nathan, "We are going to have to try to outrun him! He is still half-human…before he mutates back fully!"

I leaned into the front seat and started pounding on the horn to startle him. Luckily, it did! He backed away from the car to the middle of the road.

We immediately tried to open the doors but we couldn't.

"Oh, no! We're in a police car! The back doors will never open from the inside!" I yelled.

"Nancy! Nancy! You have to hit the unlock button and get out! Then open this door from the outside," I screamed as she sat there in shock!

"Nancy...Nancy! C'mon, it'll be ok!" I said.

Nancy cautiously unbuckled her seat belt, unlocked her door, then quietly and carefully got out of the car and grabbed our door handle.

But, just as she did, the monster saw her and lifted up the car with its tail! It began to shake it up and down like a toy! Nancy was holding on for dear life! All of a sudden one of the front tires flew off and hit the monster right in the head! It was knocked out as it dropped the car to the ground!

Nancy quickly jumped up and pulled the door open. We got out and moved to see the horrible monster lying in the middle of the road. We watched in horror as the sheriff's legs and partial face disappeared and Champ completely reappeared!

Chapter Seven - Scary

"Let's go! We have to get out of here before he wakes up!" I said.

"But...but...what about the sheriff?" asked Nancy.

"That's not the sheriff!" Nathan said.

"He's a shapeshifter...a transformer...you know, he morphed!" I said.

"What are you talking about?" asked Sissy.

I pulled my walkie-talkie out of my backpack and tried to get it to work...but we were just too far away this time.

"I'll explain later...we passed a cabin back there...maybe we can get help!" I said.

We all began running down the road and decided that it would be better if we went through the woods in case the terrifying monster woke up. There was no sign of the sheriff anywhere. I couldn't help but think that maybe that was a good thing.

The woods were dark...but luckily not too thick and we were able to run at a steady pace. We had gone about a half a mile and could see the outline of a cabin just ahead in the distance.

"I'm so tired! I need a drink of water!" said Sissy dropping to her knees as she started to take off her backpack.

"Sissy! You saw what happened to the sheriff!" I yelled.

"But you said that wasn't the sheriff!" she cried.

"Well, whatever. Okay, it wasn't. But we don't know what happened to him! We just can't stop right now!" I said as I yanked her up and we began running, catching up with Nathan and Nancy.

The wind suddenly picked up as we got closer to the cabin. It felt like some kind of weird ripple effect in the air going past us.

"What was that?" asked Nancy.

"Just a gust of wind, I guess," answered Sissy, as Nathan and I exchanged glances. We knew in our hearts that something strange and sinister had just passed by us!

Chapter Eight - Scary

As we got closer we could see the big log cabin, but it looked deserted.

"I doubt we're going to get any help in there, but maybe we can hide out." I said.

We slowly walked up the cobblestone path, past an old pond filled with croaking frogs. We went onto the huge front porch. The windows were boarded up and the front door was locked, so we went around to the back of the large deck. There we found a sliding door and it was unlocked!

We slid it open and shined our flashlights into an enormous, old, dusty cabin. As we went in, I flicked on the light switch and was happy to see that the electricity worked!

Inside was a huge rock fireplace in a room that was open to the kitchen. The furniture was covered up with old sheets and the walls were lined with animal heads.

"Wow! Somebody was either a hunter or a taxidermist." said Nathan.

"A what?" Sissy asked.

"You know, a guy who stuffs the heads of dead animals," said Nathan.

"I don't know. This place is just totally creepy!" said Sissy.

"Speaking of creepy…please tell me about this shapeshifter thing!" said Nancy.

Nathan began to explain everything he knew about shapeshifters, which was also known as transformation and metamorphosis. He told us how it's voluntary on the monster's part. It has abilities and limitations of the new form, but not the old one, which could work in reverse. And that meant we had to find out some old facts about Champ!

"Well, how?" asked Sissy.

"We are going to have to get to a library!" said Nathan.

"There is one in Port Henry, the Marcus Ridley Public Library, and it's probably still open! There's a phone! I'm going to try to call!" said Nancy as she walked over and picked it up. "It's dead."

"Everything's dead in this place!" I said.

"Maybe not!" said Sissy looking up at some of the massive stuffed animal heads.

"What do you mean?" I asked.

"Well…maybe I'm just tired, but I could swear that the eyes on that wildcat just moved!" laughed Sissy.

"RRRRRROOOOUUUUUUWWWW!!!" *We almost jumped out of our skin as the freakiest growl came from the wildcat head on the wall!*

Chapter Nine - Scary

We all spun around at once toward the horrifying sound! Right before our eyes, the head of the wildcat began to move! Its enormous sharp tooth-filled mouth opened wide as it let out another loud growl! Suddenly, it exploded out of the wall, jumping down into the middle of the room! It stood there hissing and growling at us!

It began to slowly pace the floor, stalking us! It was ready to pounce! Sissy was backing up toward the kitchen, while I slowly bent down and picked up a corner of a sheet that covered the couch. The minute I did, the ferocious cat growled and leaned toward me, showing all of its vicious teeth.

"Nathan, maybe we can cover it with this…" I spoke as calmly as I could while it watched our every move and began to pace. It was almost as if the wildcat wasn't sure which one of us to attack first. In the kitchen, Sissy had slowly picked up a huge iron skillet. And Nathan had grabbed the other corner of the sheet. We could tell it was getting restless.

"At the count of three, we'll cover him and, Sissy, use your best aim to hit him, then get down the hallway into a bedroom!" I said.

"One, two, threeeeee!" Nathan and I grabbed the corners of the sheet just as the wildcat sprang at us! Nancy took off running down the hall to find an open door while Sissy lobbed the iron skillet and hit the wild animal! But it wasn't knocked out and we could see its horrible long black claws tearing away at the sheet! We took off running down the hall!

"In here!" screamed Nancy, as we ran into the room and slammed the door and locked it! We began pulling the furniture over to the door.

Within seconds, we could hear the cat hit the door and let out a terrifying growl! It began clawing at the door!

"He's gonna claw right through! We have to go out the window!" shouted Nathan.

But the window was boarded up!

"Now what?" screamed Sissy.

"We only have seconds! That cat is mad; and it won't be a cat for long!" I said as Nathan and I opened the window, then quickly popped out the screen.

"Are you saying that the wildcat is...is...Champ?" asked Nancy.

"Exactly...but help us, you two!" said Nathan.

On the count of three we all hit the boards. They were beginning to break...but so was the door!

Chapter Ten - Scary

"Again!" I screamed, as I could see that the door was wearing away. Through the cracks we could see a mixture of fur and green scales!

We rammed the boards one last time and they broke in half! It was a long way down, but that was the least of our worries! We jumped one by one out of the window and began to run as fast as we could.

"Help!" cried Sissy. I turned to see that her backpack strap had caught on one of the boards! She was dangling from the side of the window!

"Stop!" I yelled, "we've got to help Sissy!"

Nathan and Nancy immediately stopped and we ran back toward Sissy. Within seconds, the massive cat, now transforming back into Champ, was at the window! He began swatting at her! Sissy swung back and forth like a Yo-Yo at the bottom of a string!

"Nathan, I'll distract him! You and Nancy try to pull her down."

I taunted Champ, whose long neck and enormous head came at me. We were lucky enough that his massive body was too big to fit through the window! I managed to divert his attention as he tried to push his way out! Nathan and Nancy pulled on Sissy's legs.

"You're going to have to leave your backpack behind!" yelled Nathan, "Slip your arms out of it!"

Champ heard Nathan and snapped its head back and missed chomping into Sissy by an inch! She shimmied out of her backpack and dropped to the ground! We ran as fast as our legs would go!

We heard an enormous crack as Champ had broken through the wall!

Chapter Eleven - Scary

We were a good distance ahead of him now. Luckily, his short legs couldn't travel as fast on land as they could in water. That was as long as he stayed Champ!

We finally got to Route 17, the road that had turned off from where the detour sign was, but the sign was gone! I pulled my walkie-talkie out of my backpack but it still didn't work; neither did Nathan's. Luckily, Nathan had a map.

We weren't too far from Port Henry. We knew our only hope was to get to the library and find out how to stop the horrifying shapeshifting monster!

It felt like we had been running for days! Sissy kept complaining about blisters on her feet from her new pink tennis shoes and Nancy was just quiet.

We finally passed a sign that said, 'Port Henry - Two Miles.'

"Another two miles?!" cried Sissy.

"C'mon, that thing could still be following us!" I said.

"But what do you think it wants with us?" asked Nancy.

"From what I know about transmorphing monsters is once they shapeshift when they're after you, they will spend the rest of their lives stalking you," said Nathan.

"Like, why are we trying to figure things out…can't we just go to the police, or the FBI or the National Guard??? Or anyone who can get that thing?" asked Sissy.

"No, there would be mass panic and the more people this thing sets its sights on, it could start to self-divide into numerous shapeshifters and wipe out everyone!" said Nathan.

"So, as long as it's after us, will it stay one?" I asked.

"It appears that way…but I don't want to waste too much time finding out!

We were getting closer to Port Henry. The town was deserted. We were keeping our fingers crossed that it was because everyone was watching the filming. It seemed so ironic that everyone else was looking for Champ, while we were trying desperately to get away from him! What we didn't know was that we weren't having much luck!

"Down the next street is the library," pointed Nancy.

We were out of energy but we forced ourselves to keep moving.

When we got to the library we were amazed at how historical the place was. It was a big, tall building with a steep sloping roof that went up into a straight point with red brick and stone. We ran up the steps through the huge, arched entrance and pulled on the glass doors but they were locked! Then we saw the sign.

Closed Today...
gone to see
Myth Solver Show
Come back tomorrow
Thank You!

"Don't worry! I happen to know that Mrs. Rossman hides a key in one of those magnetic boxes right here under this trash can!" Nancy said as she turned the trash can over.

"Voila!"

We quickly opened the glass door, went in and locked it again. Something about the place felt totally spooky! We walked up the inside steps into the library. The varnished oak interior and brass fixtures were original from when the place was built over one hundred years ago. The gigantic wood shelves were packed with books from floor to ceiling. In the front there was a strange looking marble statue of the man who had donated the entire library – Marcus Ridley.

We all went in different directions; Sissy and Nancy to try to find the historical records, while Nathan and I looked for books on shapeshifters.

"Here they are!" yelled Sissy, as they found massive drawers of ancient photos, maps and memorabilia. They quickly began to dig through them trying to find something on Champ.

Nathan had managed to find the rare section of books on this topic at the top of a really tall shelf. We quickly slid the ladder over to the shelf. Nathan climbed up and brought down a huge, old, black book. On the worn cloth cover in faded, gold letters it read, 'Volume 3 - Transmogrification.' We carefully opened the enormous book and turned the thick, faded, brown pages. There were some horrible drawings of humans changing into beasts, like werewolves. There were Greek myths with pictures of Athena transforming Arachne into a spider. We read about Selkies, seals who can transform from seal to human by shedding their seal skins, and then back again by pulling back on their seal coats.

Sissy and Nancy now joined us with what they found on Champ. As we flipped through the pages we were engrossed in the book but found nothing…until finally! In the back of the book there was a page that read: 'Champ - a morph'…but the page was half torn out! All that was left was a paragraph at the bottom that read…

keeping thee Champlain serpent from irrigation surrounded by of evening will bring upon extinction.

We were so engrossed reading about him, we didn't even notice the marble statue had moved!

Chapter 13 - Scary

"So, what could the missing word be?" asked Nathan.

"Don't know, but this is what we found," said Sissy as she showed us a tattered yellow piece of newspaper.

The headline read: 'Now you see him, now you don't.'

We heard a loud thump. We slowly turned around to see the marble statue standing right in front of us! He had come alive!

"AAAAGGGGHHHH!" screamed Sissy as we all ran in different directions. The statue didn't know who to run after but decided to pick me! He was horrible looking! It was the spookiest thing I had ever seen in my life! Made of heavy marble that moved with him when he ran! But the marble didn't slow him down! All of us ran to the door, but once we got there we had forgotten that we locked it!

"Quick, Nancy, the key! Give me the key!" I yelled.

"Oh, no!" she said as she searched her pockets, "I dropped it!"

Just then, the ghastly marble statue came right up to us trying to grab us while making loud moaning sounds! We ducked and crawled back into the library! He toppled over cracking the tile floor, but was back up in seconds! I turned to look and could see he was now changing back into Champ!

Nancy and Sissy were under the tables and desks frantically searching for the key, while Nathan and I tried to distract him!

"Hurry! He's beginning to change!" I screamed.

"Found it!" yelled Nancy breathlessly while she and Sissy crawled back along the tables, but the marble man was right there and he grabbed Sissy by the hair!

Sissy saw that his eyes were no longer marble but a beady yellow and swiftly poked him in the eye!

He let go of her and we grabbed her arm and pulled her with us to the door!

We managed to get out of the library, but Champ was after us and this time there was nowhere to lose him!

Chapter Fourteen - Scary

We circled around the side of a store and stopped for a second. It was dusk outside.

"That's it!" I said, pointing to the sky.

"A sunset?" questioned Sissy as she tried to catch her breath.

"No…the end of the day! Remember what the ancient book said? *Keeping thee from irrigation, of evening will bring upon extinction…* At night Champ will try heading back to water! And if we go in the opposite direction we will lose him!" We have to head toward the water but time it perfectly!" I said.

"Exactly!" shouted Nathan, "But how?" Nathan then suddenly stopped to look at his watch and the sun. He asked Nancy how many streets from where we were to the road at the beach.

"Beach Road? Just about four of five streets, then down Dock Lane!" she said.

"Perfect! C'mon, everybody, there he is!" yelled Nathan as we turned to see Champ gaining on us.

Nathan knew that if his calculations were right we would keep Champ chasing us. But we would have to make sure the sun would go down before he could get back to the water. Now that it was dusk, he could no longer shapeshift!

We ran farther down Main Street; everything was closed. We looked back and could see Champ! He wasn't far behind us! He must've known he had to get back to the water. And if we let that happen he would be stronger tomorrow and would terrorize all of Port Henry!

It was almost as if he could smell the water as we headed back on Main Street curving up past Broad Street…it seemed he was picking up speed as we headed toward Beach Road. Just like Dad always says, 'Timing is everything,' I thought to myself.

He was in hot pursuit of us now. I could see Sissy was almost collapsing.

"We're almost there…it's almost over!" I yelled as the sun was setting. We were turning down Dock Lane and the ferocious lake monster was now weaving and barely standing up! We were just a few feet away from the end of Dock Lane to Beach Road when Champ fell. The monster got back up, only to fall flat a few more feet away. Now it was time to use our walkie-talkies.

We stopped where we were, while waiting to see if it would get up again. Champ began to crawl, but collapsed!

We all fell to the ground from complete exhaustion yet thrilled to be alive!

"Mom? Mom? Over!" I said.

"Mick? Mick, where have you been? I have been worried sick about you and tried to reach you all day! Over," she said.

"I know. Our walkie-talkies wouldn't work. Over."

"Oh! I told the cable company not to get these new-fangled things. Anyway, where are you? The crew is just breaking down. Over."

"Mom. I think they might need to keep those cameras rolling. Over," I said, as I gave her directions to where we were.

Chapter Fifteen - Scary

Sirens were sounding as tons of police cars and the Myth Mobile pulled up. Nobody could believe their eyes! Our parents and the crew ran over and hugged us! We were so happy to see them! The crew set up to film.

"Don't you move an inch out of my site!" said Mom as she took her place in front of the camera.

"Not an inch!" said Dad as he messed up my already messed up hair.

The police officers had secured the lake monster as the cameras started to roll. Mom and Dad played it off as even more of a mystery as to how this lake monster had washed up on shore when the tide was going out.

They wrapped up the shoot and came over to us.

"Odd how it looks like it is heading toward the water and not out of it," said Dad as we walked to the Myth Mobile.

"Well, it's a really, really long story, Dad." I said.

"Well, son, we've got all night," he replied as we all boarded the Myth Mobile, including the sheriff and deputies.

We told everyone what happened but they found it hard to believe. But immediately they called the state police and the other sheriff's office in Vermont and set out to investigate.

By the next day they found the other sheriff and he was alive!

They also found Sissy's backpack, the hole in the wall at the boarded up cabin, and the broken statue in the library.

The crew and Mom and Dad wrapped up the show.

Phone calls poured in from across the world and reporters were combing the little town of Port Henry. We had to pose for *Persons* magazine and a bunch more. Sissy was in her glory and Nancy was a hometown hero!

Even though they found the entire story hard to believe, it had been the most successful myth solving mission ever!

Because the truth about the shapeshifting Champ had been uncovered!

An Ever Changing Ending!

Chapter One - Freakish Fairy Tale

Once upon a time Port Henry, New York, was the most beautiful town in all the land. It was surrounded by green pastures, magnificent orchards and great forests. Yet, the crowning glory of this tiny hamlet was the mysterious Lake Champlain.

Although the lake had provided a busy port to the foreign worlds, it also housed a deep dark secret – one the king was well aware of.

You see, many, many, moons ago, his son, Prince Mickers, his niece, Lady Sissyelia, and his nephew, Lord Nathan, and a strange girl who navigated the boat…had been out on the lake and had encountered a horrible accident as the boat had crashed to shore…thrown by a mysterious mystical beast!

Now he sat on his throne surrounded by his loyal court, pondering what to do. Fear was brewing in the land.

Prince Mickers and the king's men, Lord Nathan, Sir Hinkelson, Sir Brett, and all the other loyal knights had gone on a myth solving crusade. They had traveled through the woods to board the ship – The Uncoververia – months ago, determined to slay the cunning beast.

The same Champ that Sir Mickers and Lord Nathan had encountered, an enormous lake monster that hid in the deepest darkest depths of the lake. A beast so vile and brutal it would shoot fire from its mouth, toasting everything within its path, then devouring it like a crumpet.

For the few who had seen the ruthless monster, it was said to be of great enormity; with a huge body, a dragon-like head with rows of dagger-sharp teeth, fins with curving three foot long claws and a long thick tail. But even more frightening was its neck! It was so long it could wrap completely around any seagoing vessel and crush it!

The harbor had long been quiet as the rumors of Champ had spread through the land. Ships no longer came to the port, so the villagers had nobody to trade with. They were forced to farm and fish for every bit of their food. Things were growing grim for the town of Port Henry. Prince Mickers knew if he didn't finish off the lake monster the worst would truly happen.

Now the town was becoming restless. They no longer trusted the king, because their beliefs were swayed by the vicious Lord Wantsalot. He had convinced the villagers that the king and his court were wasting their precious duty money on silly lake monster expeditions.

The king was afraid that if Prince Mickers and his knights didn't return from their mission soon, he would lose control of his village. And worse than that, his throne.

And he was right!

For many moons, the evil Lord Wantsalot shrewdly enticed many farmers into selling their farmlands and fisherman into selling their boats. Lord Wantsalot offered them such a high fare that the villagers fell into his hands with their greed for money, thus selling him all of their farms and boats.

Once Lord Wantsalot owned everything that brought in food, he slowly began to cut them off. He would sell them just enough food to keep them alive…and at ridiculously high prices; an ear of corn for 750 pence, an apple for 800 pence and a half a fish for 900 pence.

By charging such high prices, Lord Wantsalot eventually had all of the money he had paid to them to buy their boats and farms back into his greedy pockets. But that wasn't the end of it. Once their money was gone he demanded their jewels for food, too! Pretty soon, the king had to help by giving up the royal jewels just to feed his people! One by one, an emerald for a stalk of celery, a diamond for an onion, or a ruby for a tomato, until the castle was now empty of its riches!

As the people slowly began getting hungrier and weaker, they grew irritable, unhappy and poor! The king kept trying to feed the people with the castle's meager harvest, and by giving up the castle's royal jewels, but it was no use; the supply had run out!

All the while, Lord Wantsalot secretly assembled a troupe of the most vicious shrewd evil-doers in all the land, while planning a cruel takeover of the town and throne!

He had planned to marry Lady Sissyelia, Prince Mickers' cousin, and the only remaining eligible girl to the throne. If Lord Wantsalot could end the reign of the king and queen, and conquer Prince Mickers – he would force Lady Sissyelia to be his bride! Then he would become the king and reign with terror! *A terror the people had never known!*

"Open up! I say…open up!" said the evil voice.

Maiden Nancy cowered silently in the corner of her tiny cabin as they pounded on her door. She knew if she opened the door, Lord Wantsalot's vicious soldiers would find her hen and demand that she sell it to them; or even worse…her magic rubies!

Maiden Nancy had managed to survive without having to sell her goods – but now her time had run out!

She held her breath as she stood silently. She had secretly hoped they wouldn't bother her because she was known as 'Crazy Maiden Nancy.' The villagers had dubbed her that because she had always longed to be a knight and had ventured to town many times to the knight tryouts at the castle – only to be ridiculed. She knew now – this would be her chance!

The banging on the door finally stopped as she peeked out the window. She could see the evil men in her garden stealing all of her vegetables! They mounted their horses and took off toward town. She had heard about the rumors, but now knew it to be true!

She knew what she had to do! If she didn't find Prince Mickers to let him know what was happening to the town, Lord Wantsalot would rule the land!

Once she was certain the evil men had left, she moved a chair to a shelf high up on the wall. She then carefully took the middle book and opened it. It was hollowed out inside, and in it was a black leather pouch. She untied the leather pouch and lifted out the beautiful gold locket. She opened the locket to reveal six rubies, three that glistened so brightly they lit up the room, and three dull. She closed the locket, undid the clasp and put the necklace on.

Next she packed her Myth Solver satchel, locked up her tiny cabin, jumped on her horse, and headed into the deep dark forest surrounding Lake Champlain.

It was near dusk and she knew she had only a short time to find Prince Mickers before nightfall. The darker it grew outside, the scarier the forest got! It was almost as if it took on a life of its own; the trees began to look like black stick figures moving in the wind. The leaves would rustle as if someone were there. Owls began to hoot, and bats would swoop down at Maiden Nancy as she grew more and more terrified!

"Giddy-yap…c'mon boy!" she said as she tried to get her horse to move faster. But the darker it grew, the more skittish the horse became.

"Hoooooot!!!" An owl startled the horse so badly it reared up on its hind legs knocking Maiden Nancy to the ground! *Then the horse galloped away in fear!*

"Did thine heareth that?" Prince Mickers asked.

"All I can heareth is this delicious turkey!" said Sir Hinkelson as he tore a leg right off the hot barbecue spit.

"No, listen!" stated Prince Mickers.

"It sounds like an animal cometh!" said Lord Nathan, as he and Prince Mickers walked toward the edge of camp.

Prince Mickers and his knights were exhausted. They had lost their ship in Lake Champlain to Champ. The horrible monster had circled its giant neck around the ship so tightly they all had to escape by jumping off and swimming to shore. Luckily they had all made it, but the king's ship was gone, as well as any way in or out of Port Henry! The beast would grow hungry and they knew it would follow them! Now they had to get back to town to warn of the coming of the evil lake monster, Champ!

As Prince Mickers and Lord Nathan got to the edge of the woods, there was a lone stallion grazing.

"Here boy…easy there, boy…" said Prince Mickers, as he and Lord Nathan surrounded the horse and grabbed the reins of the stallion.

"I say, that stallion belongs to Crazy Maiden Nancy!" stated Sir Brett as he walked up.

"Why do they call her Crazy Maiden Nancy?" asked Lord Nathan.

"Because the maiden claims she owneth magic rubies that could feed a nation or bring death to a lake monster – whatever she commands them to do, aside from the fact that she wants to become a knight!" shrugged Sir Brett.

"Well, I can understand why they thinketh the woman has lost her senses!" answered Lord Nathan, as they brought the stallion closer to camp.

The camp broke out in massive laughter until Prince Mickers spoke.

"Well, what if thine maiden is telling the truth?" he asked.

"Magic rubies and a woman becoming a knight? Really, Prince Mickers, what thinketh thou?"

They all laughed until suddenly the wind picked up and the ground shook!

"I feel the earth move under my feet and the sky tumbling down!" screamed Prince Mickers! Until he realized it was Champ!

"The beast has grown land legs! We have to get back to town!" he hollered.

Champ was on the move and it would devour and burn anything in its path.

As they quickly mounted their horses and began to head back toward town, Prince Mickers grabbed the reins of Crazy Maiden Nancy's stallion. But the stallion was stubborn and insisted on going a different way through the woods!

"Go ahead, warn my father and the villagers of the impending doom!" yelled Prince Mickers.

The ground shook as Champ got closer!

"I'm going with thou!" hollered Lord Nathan.

Prince Mickers shook his head 'no', as the stallion pulled him and his horse in a different direction. But he knew it was no use arguing with his best friend. They began galloping off the path and through the dense forest letting the stallion lead the way.

Once into the darkest part of the forest the stallion stopped. The woods were silent.

"Nathan, whereth are we?" asked Prince Mickers holding up the torch while trying to see.

"I do not know, sire. I have never been through this part of the forest," answered Lord Nathan.

"Freeze and put your hands upeth, or I will pummel you in the wind!" screamed a woman's voice. "Who goes there?!"

"I am Prince Mickers," he said as they froze in their tracks.

"Oh! Forgive me, your highness, I didn't know it was you!" exclaimed Maiden Nancy as she popped up from under a bed of leaves startling them.

"And you have my horse!" she exclaimed.

"Yes…it's you! The girl who commandeered our fated boats many moons ago! Come quickly…there's no time!" stated Prince Mickers, "Champ, the vicious lake monster, has done what I have always feared…it has grown land legs!"

But what they didn't know was that Champ was only part of the problem!

"Hide Lady Sissyelia and the queen in the tower! We will have to surrender before they burn down the castle!" the king yelled to his court.

There was nothing he could do! Lord Wantsalot with his evil doers was now overthrowing the castle! He had pushed the entire village into anger and famine! Since most of the king's knights were out with Prince Mickers, the king, his court, and the few knights who had stayed behind were outnumbered!

As he looked down over the top of the castle, he could see the people had gone crazy with hunger. Lord Wantsalot was now in charge, commanding his vicious followers to bridge the castle's moat, preparing to break down the castle door!

The king ordered the remaining knights to open the door as he took his place on his throne surrounded by his court. Within seconds, Lord Wantsalot and his evil doers were inside the castle.

"Where art thou, Lady Sissyelia?" Lord Wantsalot demanded as he approached the king.

The king and his court remained silent.

"Ohh, I see…not speaking are we? Bound and gag them if they won't speak and throw them in the dungeon!" ordered Lord Wantsalot.

His villains quickly followed his commands and grabbed the king and his court, and threw them in the dungeon! He then ordered all the townspeople back to their homes. The sinister Lord Wantsalot would trick Prince Mickers!

When he and his men returned it would appear as if nothing in the town had changed! It would be the last group Lord Wantsalot would overthrow. But in his haste, he neglected to think about Champ…

Prince Mickers, Lord Nathan and Maiden Nancy quickly mounted their horses and caught up with the rest of the knights.

On the way back, Maiden Nancy told them of the impending doom in the village. It was a horrifying night, as they would soon face the wicked Lord Wantsalot…while being followed by Champ, which was now a blood-curdling land monster! Somehow, Prince Mickers was going to have to come up with a plan.

Upon entering town, they could feel the chill in the air. Even though it was dark, except for the few burning torches guiding the way, they could feel the eyes upon them peeking through the doors. When they would glance toward the homes, doors would slam and windows would shut.

"I can feel they have already overthrown the castle!" whispered Prince Mickers, fearfully.

"But we can useth my magic rubies…" began Maiden Nancy.

"Right-o, we'll do that," interrupted Lord Nathan as he rolled his eyes.

"I know thine does not believe me…as nobody believed in a lake monster either," quipped Nancy.

When they got to the front of the castle it was dark; all of the torches were out. Then the enormous wood and metal gate slowly lowered over the moat, as they cautiously entered the dark castle.

Once inside the castle gates it was a nightmare! They were immediately pulled off their horses!

In the scuttle, Maiden Nancy quickly took off her necklace and opened the locket while covering the glow from the magic rubies. She put the three regular rubies into her hand and closed the locket with the remaining rubies in it, and quickly tucked it into her pocket. And just in time! They had lost the struggle and were tied up and thrown into the ballroom!

"I thought this would be a good place for you to viewth my wedding!" growled Lord Wantsalot as he sat on the throne, running his hand through a massive bag of jewels.

"Your wedding?! And who would marry you?" yelled Prince Mickers.

"Well, whomever I chooseth…but it just so happens I choose Lady Sissyelia! That's who!" Lord Wantsalot said as he walked over and got face to face with Prince Mickers.

"You can then watcheth as I become the new king! HAHAHAHAHA!" his evil laugh echoed through the silence. "Yes, lovely Lady Sissyelia, who is hidden in the tower! You will now then tellth me where the key to the tower is, OR YOU WILL NEVER SPEAKETH AGAIN!!!"

screamed Lord Wantsalot at the top of his lungs, while he attached the massive bag of jewels to his hip.

"I see y…y…you enjoy your jewels!" stuttered Maiden Nancy.

"SILENCE!" howled Lord Wantsalot whipping his head around to look at Maiden Nancy.

"I will give you my magic rubies…if you promise no harm will come to the royal family!" yelled Maiden Nancy.

"Rubies, ahhh…yes, it is Crazy Maiden Nancy and her fantastical made up ruby story," said Lord Wantsalot menacingly walking toward Maiden Nancy.

"They are right here in my hand," she said.

Lord Wantsalot pulled a glistening sharp sword from his side and quickly cut the ropes that bound Maiden Nancy's hands behind her. She slowly opened her hand to reveal three fake rubies.

He grabbed them out of her hand then laughed and yelled. "Foolish girl! Tie her up again!"

But before anyone could get to her there was an enormous yell…

"AAAAARRRGGGGHHHHOOOUUUNNNN!"

It was followed by screams and chaos from beyond the castle walls!

"Champ…it's Champ!" I screamed, as the evil men began to run to the windows.

Maiden Nancy was still untied as she slowly backed away while motioning for us to be quiet. She then quickly dashed up the castle stairs toward the tower.

They could see by the torches the shadow of an enormous beast! As they watched in fear, Champ entered the village and was headed straight down the thoroughfare toward the castle with fire shooting out of its mouth!

"Get the canons! We will blow the beast to smithereens!" hollered Lord Wantsalot, as his nasty men dashed around gathering up weapons!

Maiden Nancy was out of breath as she reached the top of the steps in the tower.

"Lady…Sissyelia!" she said.

The tiny slot in the heavy bolted metal door slowly slid open.

"And who are you?" asked the queen, as she peered out of the hole, while hiding Lady Sissyelia behind her.

"I have no time to explain, but Prince Mickers is in the castle, just come with me!" said Maiden Nancy.

"How can we trust you?" asked the queen.

"You simply must! I found Prince Mickers on the expedition on Lake Champlain…" Maiden Nancy babbled while trying to convince the queen.

"Even if you are who you say, we have no key," answered the queen.

Maiden Nancy quickly pulled the locket out of her pocket and carefully took a sparkling ruby out, placed it into the lock, and said something under her breath. Within seconds, the door to the tower vanished. She grabbed their hands and they ran down the tall, thin, curving stone stairs as she told her story and the plan.

When they reached the bottom of the stairs there was total chaos! It was easy for the queen and Lady Sissyelia to hide as Maiden Nancy took out another ruby and rolled it toward the group of tied up men while muttering under her breath. Instantly the ropes undid themselves!

The more they continued to fight off Champ, the angrier he got! He had chomped off a giant piece of the castle's stone wall and now his enormously long neck was wrapping in and out of the castle windows! It was completely stretched, then recoiled!

But Lord Wantsalot got sidetracked when he turned around and caught a glimpse of Lady Sissyelia peeking out from behind a massive wooden chair! He immediately ordered two of his men to go to the dungeon and get the monarch to marry him!

But he would have to fight Prince Mickers and his men to get to Lady Sissyelia as they jumped up the minute they were free.

There was fighting everywhere!

"Move out of my way, Prince Mickers! You do want to be present when I marry your cousin, Lady Sissyelia," laughed Lord Wantsalot as he drew his sword, "because I am going to marryeth her right now!!! Ha, Ha, Ha, Ha, Ha!" he bellowed…but only a bit too soon!

"Never!" screamed Prince Mickers, as he grabbed a torch from the wall and waved it at Lord Wantsalot, while defending the queen and Lady Sissyelia.

Fire blazed through the front gate as Champ was burning down the door!

"A ruby, Maiden Nancy! Quickly!" yelled Prince Mickers…but just as Maiden Nancy pulled the very last ruby out of her locket and tossed it toward Prince Mickers…Champ's massive head came exploding through the door!

The ruby flew through the air as it glistened in the candlelight. It was headed right toward Prince Mickers; Champ spotted the ruby, swooped his massive head and neck right for it and gobbled it down!

Maiden Nancy immediately sprang forward toward Champ and said,

> "Champ, lake monster I send a ruby to thee,
> to eat the one who has the regular three.
> His evil self who willed the town poor,
> will do evil nevermore, nevermore…
> And once digested in you, massive beast,
> for you, too, shall fall,
> providing the town with a massive feast!"

Then Champ slowly turned as if he was going right toward Maiden Nancy!

But he passed right by her and went straight for Lord Wantsalot! Lord Wantsalot screamed and began to run, but he couldn't go too fast because he was so weighed down by all the heavy jewels in the bag attached to his belt!

Then came a horrible site! Lord Wantsalot, jewels and all, were swallowed up and you could see them going down,

down, down all the way to the bottom of Champ's long, skinny neck – whole!

Champ looked at everyone and let out a gigantic burp!

As we began backing away, the horrible lake monster began to stagger. He tried to walk, but swayed from side to side. Then suddenly it jerked upright, spun around, and fell backwards outside with a thud!

Seconds later, there was a thunderous roar outside the castle!!!

The noise came from people running in the streets screaming, cheering and applauding with joy! Champ was dead!

We quickly rounded up the sinister followers of Lord Wantsalot and threw them into the dungeon, while giving freedom to the king and his court!

The king went outside to inspect Champ and to proclaim that the evil doers were safely locked away and that food, safety and peace would once again be restored to Port Henry!

They planned to have an enormous feast of roasted Champ fish the next day!

"Nice work, Maiden Nancy!" exclaimed Prince Mickers…" I think thou have earned thine knighthood!"

"Seriously!" added Lord Nathan as he bowed to her.

Maiden Nancy smiled as Lady Sissyelia walked up to join them while they laughed and cheered.

At daybreak, the town was decorated in its finest flags! Champ was now turning on an enormous spit and being served up on giant plates. We took our places at the banquet. Trumpets sounded as the king and queen entered and took their places.

154

"It is now time to have some Champ fish, remember first to pick out jewels to be yours from this delicious rich dish! As we are done with thou evil ones! It is now time to have some fun!" the king proclaimed.

As everyone got their slab of Champ fish they picked out many jewels! Everyone shared their wealth as they ate their way back to prosperity and good health…as they all lived and laughed happily ever after!

The End of the Fish Tale

We were holding on for our lives as we flew through the air in the boat! Suddenly, the boat began to tilt down toward the water, turning to one side! It was tipping over!

The boat was turning completely upside down! We couldn't hold on any longer! *Splashhhh! Splashhhh! Splashhhh!* Each one of us fell into the water and then *Fwwwwaaaammmp!!!!* The boat hit the water hard! Causing a huge wave!

I came up and began treading water while trying to see, but it was still dark out!

"Nathan…*glug…glug*… Sissy!...*blurp*…Nancy!" I screamed at the top of my lungs while trying not to take in big gulps of water! I managed to stay on the surface but the waves were high! *"Don't panic! Don't panic!"* I said to myself, knowing it was the worse thing you could do in an emergency situation!

Maybe everyone was on the other side of the boat, even though it seemed impossible because the boat had hit the water about 20 feet from where we fell!

I began to swim toward the capsized boat. It was all I could do to keep going. I was just thankful we all had our life vests on, *but where were they?*

As I got closer to the boat, I felt a tug pulling at my feet and I freaked out...Champ! He was still in these waters! What if he had gotten Sissy, Nathan and Nancy?!

I was terrified but I had to keep it together!... *Then I felt another tug!*

Chapter Two - Sci-Fi

Something was trying to pull me under water! The next thing I knew, both my feet were pulled together – I couldn't stay up! It was as if I was caught in a vacuum and being sucked down!

Seconds later, I was in a dark, sleek black metal tube being pulled downward at super speed!

It was the scariest and most puzzling thing that had ever happened to me. My hands were at my sides; the tube was the size of a waterslide…in fact, it was just like a waterslide as it curved and twisted…my backpack hitting the sides, going down…down…down…then there was a wide opening and BAM!

I hit the bottom!

"Mick…Mick! Dude! You're all right!" yelled familiar voices!

When I looked up, I was thrilled to see Sissy, Nathan and Nancy! We all stood up and began to hug…then quickly stopped, backed away from each other and shook it off!

"What the heck?" I asked, dazed as I looked around the small round chamber that was lit up by an eerie blue glow, "Where in the world are we?"

"All I know is that we were sucked out of the water into this tube thingy!" replied Sissy.

"Yeah, like some sort of metal vacuum – nothing I've ever seen before!" answered Nathan.

Now I knew we were in trouble! If Nathan didn't have any answers, the rest of us wouldn't either! I stood up and began tapping the walls, but it was just a hollow metal sound that echoed.

The others joined in as we began to tap on every panel, but it just seemed to be heavy metal that was bolted together by massive steel.

"Maybe we can get out the same way we came in," said Sissy.

Nathan and I went and looked up the tube we had dropped down from, but there was no way to get up to it and it was so long, it just seemed endless.

"Not likely," I replied.

"NOT LIKELY..." *click, click* "INDEED!" bellowed a strange, scary voice that sounded like teeth clicking in between words, its frightening sound echoed throughout the chamber.

We all froze!

"What was that?" quivered Sissy, as we all looked around the mysterious place.

"Don't know…" I whispered, as chills ran up and down my spine.

"IT'S NOT POLITE TO WHISPER!!!" snapped the hollow voice.

We all looked at each other, totally afraid.

"Who…who are you?" I asked, while trying to sound as composed as possible.

"It doesn't matter who I am. What matters is what you want with Champ," the voice snidely responded.

"Champ? What could this possibly have to do with Champ?" asked Nancy.

"Isn't that what I just asked you?" the evil voice responded.

Nathan was now circling the room and he suddenly pointed to a small speaker at the top of the frightening chamber, right where the voice was coming from!

"Who are you and what do you want with us?" I asked, as I walked closer to the speaker.

"BACK AWAY!" screamed the voice.

I was startled for a second, but I stood my ground repeating, "Who are you and what do you want with us?"

"Ahhh…" *click, click* "a feisty little Myth Solver are you?" The voice answered back, "I will tell you in due time, in due time!" Then there was a click and silence.

"He, whatever it is, must have a camera in that speaker too, and is probably watching our every move," said Nathan.

"I want to get out of here right now!" cried Sissy.

We were all really frightened. Somehow this crazy person had sucked us into some kind of horrible metal prison with no possible way out!

Chapter Four - Sci-Fi

We paced inside the mysterious, metal chamber wondering what to do. The entire place had a weird feeling to it, almost as if it was floating. Sometimes there were metal creaks and then suddenly there was pounding.

"What was that?" asked Sissy.

"I don't know," I said, as I motioned for everyone to huddle up. We got into a very tight circle, so we could talk without the voice hearing us...

"Listen, we can't just stay and wait. We need to get out of here," I whispered.

"Mick's right. Let's try to talk as little as possible and only use hand motions. Who has their digital camera? I have an idea!" said Nathan.

Sissy raised her hand, took off her backpack, opened it and pulled out her camera. While hiding it, she slid it to Nathan.

He motioned for us to circle up again and asked for ropes and hooks.

We got all the supplies together we needed as secretly as we could, while the freaky place we were in continued to creak and sway.

We tested the speaker and realized we were not being watched at the moment, as Nathan quickly directed us to pose. He then placed the camera on our backpacks, set the timer and swiftly joined us in a pose for the picture.

"EEEEEAAAAHHH, EEEEEAAAAHHH, EEEEEAAAAHHH…" An ear-deafening siren sounded! It must have been set off by the flash! It was so loud we covered our ears in pain! Nathan quickly leapt on top of the camera to hide it! While trying to cover our ears we formed a block in front of him! We knew it would be only seconds and whoever, or whatever, would be watching us again!

It seemed like the siren went on for days, then it finally shut off. But next came the eerie teeth-gnashing voice.

"Have you done something I should" *click, click* "know about, you nasty little beings?"

We stood there silent as Nathan slowly got up and joined us.

"I SAID…" it screeched, as I interrupted him.

"We haven't done anything," I said.

SNAP, again the sound of the speaker went dead.

We didn't move for a few minutes. Then, when we knew the coast was clear, we continued with our plan. Nathan picked up the camera, checking to make sure he had gotten the shot; while we tied the hooks to the rope and tossed it up to the screened speaker. It caught!

We grabbed the rope and yanked the screen off. Very carefully, Nancy and Sissy kneeled down right next to the wall under the speaker, while I kneeled on top of them. We were making a cheerleader pyramid, Nathan had to move carefully and quickly as he stood on my back.

"Ouuch! Like, you're killing me!" snapped Sissy.

"Be quiet, if you really don't want something killing you!" I said.

Sissy stopped at that thought…we were working against time now. Once up there, Nathan quickly attached our digital camera to the video camera that had been watching us. Suddenly he began motioning frantically. I tried to look up.

Then he pulled his carabiner off his belt loop and hooked it into the small square area where the camera was. He then lifted his feet off me and braced himself against the wall and pulled. We jumped up and helped by pulling on him.

CLANK! We all tumbled down to the floor, as instantly a hidden door opened up…but a door to where?

We slowly made our way to the door, but jumped a mile as the eerie voice clicked from the speaker.

"I see you are not as motivated to get out as I thought! Ha, ha, ha, hahhh!" CLICK.

We were petrified with fear, until we realized the door remained open! He had been looking at the motionless picture on the digital camera! It worked! We looked at each other and clapped silently. It was hard not to break out laughing as we looked at each other applauding like we were a bunch of mimes.

We gained our composure back and slowly made our way into the deep, winding, perilous hallway. It was a long, gloomy corridor. Kind of like a tunnel, the entire thing was just like the area we came from – sleek, shiny dark metal with bolts in it.

All of a sudden the entire thing jerked, then it felt like it was moving!

"Mick, are you thinking what I'm thinking?" Nathan questioned.

"Yeah. We are under water…" I whispered.

"Under water?" Sissy blurted out nervously.

"Shhhh," I said, as I swallowed hard.

We continued to creep through the halls looking for some sort of a way out, or a sign, just something; but the place was completely lifeless. We continued down the dark hallways until we realized we had just gone in one gigantic circle.

"Mick, he's going to come looking for us soon!" said Sissy.

"I know," I replied.

"Well, why don't we try some of those big, huge doors we walked past?" Sissy asked.

"That's a great idea, Sissy, should we just walk in and if someone is there, say 'Oops, sorry, don't mind us, just looking for the exit…" I barked.

"Alright guys, this is getting us nowhere," said Nathan, and before he could get the words out of his mouth, one of the huge doors began to open – very slowly.

We ducked around the side of the hallway, pushing ourselves against the wall as tightly as possible. What we saw next was totally weird! It was a robot! But not an ordinary robot! It looked like it was made of a shiny silver liquid; the way it moved, gliding along in one solid piece with no creases anywhere! It stared straight ahead; there was no nose, no mouth…just round, hollow, black eyes! It wasn't human!

We watched the weird thing slink across the hallway to another door. As it stood in front of the massive metal door, it immediately opened automatically. The robot went in, but the door remained open!

"We have got to see what's in there!" I said.

"C'mon, I'm with you!" said Nathan as they ducked across the hall.

"Stop, you two! It could be a trap!" said Sissy, but her curiosity was more than she could handle, as Nancy and Sissy followed closely behind us.

We couldn't believe our eyes. It was a massive sized room. As we peered in we could see a long, skinny curving metal staircase the robot was slowly going down. But one level below was even more shocking…it was a giant lab!

There were giant sized coils that bounced electrical currents back and forth, walls of computers and generators, and huge glass beakers that had all kinds of glowing purple liquid in them!

An even bigger shock was that from a giant glass window we could see we were completely under water!

"Where are we?" asked Sissy.

"It looks like we are at the bottom of Lake Champlain!" I whispered.

"But what is this place?" asked Nancy.

"I would say it is an underwater laboratory…and my guess is they are doing something illegal!" I answered.

"Yeah…I would say kidnapping is illegal…" added Sissy.

From the window we could see the enormity of the place; long metal tubes welded together that seemed to extend into different sections. They went in a large circle, but in the middle, in the open water area, nestled in the sandy bottom of the lake, were enormous clear pods that glowed an eerie purple!

It looked like some kind of experiment, but we didn't have time to check it out…

Swish, swish, swish…the disturbing robot was coming back up the stairs.

"Quick…under the table!" I yelled, as we all dove for it, then quickly scooted around to the other side of some cabinets as it exited the room. We listened for the heavy metal door to close.

Once we heard it rattle shut, we knew it was safe, so we began to look around. Nathan started checking out the computers, while I went to the desk and began reading the notes and papers to try to figure out what was going on.

"This is interesting…" said Sissy as she pointed up above the desk.

There was an old company sign that read, ARRITANE TECHNOLOGIES - DELIVERIES IN BACK. The sign looked like it had been broken and then someone took red spray paint and drew the international 'NO' symbol around it.

"Arritane Technologies? That was an old company that was based in Burlington, just on the other side of the lake in Vermont," said Nancy excitedly.

"Really? Are they still there?" I asked.

"No, and it's a really weird story…" Nancy said quietly, then slowly began to explain. Nothing could have been more bizarre than what happened next!

Chapter Eight - Sci-Fi

The entire place shook for a second as the lights blinked on and off! Instantly, we could see what appeared to be massive headlights coming toward us from outside the giant window!

We ran and hid. But even odder than that was the headlights were on what appeared to be a massive Champ!

"Nathan, do you see what I see?" my voice shook.

"I think so…are you seeing Champ with headlights for eyes?" he asked.

Crouched down, we scooted closer to the window for a better look. It was surreal as we watched the massive beast!

Then, it seemed like the gigantic lake monster was attaching itself to one of the tunnels on the huge underwater structure!

"That's not a real lake monster…" exclaimed Nancy.

"It's a robot!" Nathan and I whispered together.

It was like a submarine, only covered with dinosaur-like skin and features shaped in the form of Champ! Now we were going to have to find out what was going on, while trying to find a way out of this creepy place!

"Nancy, tell us what you know about Arritane Technologies…" Nathan said, while we began to look in cabinets and drawers, combing the place for more information.

"Well, from what I remember, they were manufacturers on the cutting edge of liquid-based products they were developing to work as some kind of a spray shield…One of their scientists had a major breakthrough and he came up with a liquid that nothing could penetrate…kind of like a bulletproof vest. But you would just spray this liquid on your clothes," Nancy explained.

"I read about that!" said Nathan, "in one of my magazines."

"You probably did, it was all over the news…because something was wrong with the formula and the finished product left a dangerous toxic liquid after they sprayed it on. The plant was ordered to stop making it. This was years ago, and the company was forced to shut down. Then all kinds of weird things started happening…" continued Nancy.

"Like what?" asked Sissy enthusiastically.

"Well, the plant was situated right on the lake and sometimes at night the lights would be on and there would be loud noises…but the place was abandoned. Then, things from the deserted plant, like barrels and metal tubes, would be found floating on the lake. All the remaining metal parts and tubes were stolen!

171

They say the guy who developed the formula, who was supposed to destroy it, disappeared. People said it was his life's work and that he had gone insane!

"Really?" *Click, click...*"Is that what they said about me?" said the evil voice from behind us!

We jumped at the sound of the voice. "What's the matter, little Miss Yacker," *click, click*…"Cat got your tongue?" he asked.

As we slowly turned to see the madman, Nancy screamed, turned pale white and fainted!

We patted her on the face as I dug out a water bottle and gave her a sip.

"I hate weaklings!" *Click...click…* "I should feed her to the fish!" said the weird looking man!

He was a short elderly man with dirty, grayish-blond hair with black streaks running through it, and it stood up on end.

He had thick black round glasses smashed into his hair and an evil wrinkled face with a pointy nose and watery red eyes. His crooked teeth were small and looked like they were cut from his clicking them when he talked. He was wearing a dirty lab coat and rumpled grey pants with tennis shoes.

Nancy woke up, but was woozy as we helped her stand. She stared at the man as he looked right at her and said, "Insane? Maybe…but your story doesn't stop there…" *click, click*, "I have developed a formula that will change the world…and I will own it!" he yelled and then clapped his hands as two identical robots swiftly appeared.

"Look at their beautiful sleek skin. I made it myself and it will repel anything! I have created this underwater fortress…" *click, click*, "and I will control everything! See my beautiful toxic garden…" *click click*, "those lovely specimens will keep predators away! Predators like you!"

"Run!" I yelled and we all bolted for the door, but the scientist just clapped his hands again and the two robots blocked the door!

"Run where? Once you're an intruder…" *click, click*, "you must stay!"

"But, we weren't intruding!" I yelled, "you sucked us in!"

"You were intruding in my lake with your silly myth solving family! Lock them up!"

"But, we were just trying to see Champ, you know how I feel about Champ!" Nancy said tearfully.

"Champ! Ha! How silly…people who believe in myths deserve to suffer! Ha, ha, ha! See…" *click, click,* "you Myth Solver people shouldn't put your noses where they don't belong!" he snapped.

The two robots followed his exact command as he told them to lock us up. They forced us into a giant metal cage that was sitting on a glass panel opening to the water below!

"Nancy, are you okay?" I asked.

"Yeah, you fainted for a sec. You look pale!" said Sissy.

"Fine, fine. Yeah, I'm fine…it's, it's, well, I'm f-f-fine," she stuttered.

"I have only read about this stuff in science fiction books!" whispered Nathan, as we watched the madman work in his lab while the robots stood guard.

"Do you remember anything about this at all, Nathan, what you read? Anything? Or do you, Nancy?" I whispered.

"I remember the toxins were made of gaseous liquid and they were worried about their containment because of the harm they would do…" whispered Nathan, as he slowly pointed at the large glass pods that contained glowing purple liquid outside of the massive underwater lab.

"Yeah, from the rumors I heard around town, when everything was happening at the factory, the formula was stolen right after he disappeared," said Nancy.

"Is that him?" I asked.

Nancy slowly nodded.

"You're sure?" I asked.

"Positive," answered Nancy, "he's older, and I think something happened to his teeth – from the newspaper pictures…that my grandfather had kept."

"Why did your grandfather keep them?" I asked.

"Because, uh…he worked at the plant," she whispered, "But even if we escape, what about those toxic chemicals? It's clear he's crazy. Those chemicals have to be destroyed, too, or they will kill everything within 5,000 miles of this place."

We quickly stopped talking as the crazy scientist walked over to listen.

Click, click… then he turned and went back to his desk.

"What are we going to do?" Sissy asked.

By now Nathan had sat down and was scribbling a bunch of notes on his small notepad from his backpack. Nancy joined him as they continued to talk about chemicals, while acting as if they were shaking them. It was strange scientific stuff I didn't understand, but I knew they were up to something.

"Guard them…and don't move!" the madman snapped, "I'll be back."

This would probably be our only chance to escape! I had a feeling these were the only two robots in the place, and I doubted very much that there was anyone else, just this madman and his two robots.

"Do you have any rope in your backpack?" Nathan asked.

"Like, I have a jump rope!" replied Sissy.

"A jump rope? What kind of Myth Solver gear is that?" I asked.

"Never mind... that'll work, Sissy. Get it," said Nathan, and when he turned away she stuck her tongue out at me.

All I could think of was, 'how did I ever get into these situations with her?!'

"Mick, you ready for some lock picking?" I nodded, as I knew exactly what he meant while I pulled out my special key tool. I had gotten it when a tow truck guy had helped my dad. He had forgot about the key and left it."

"Now, we need one more rope," said Nathan, just as Nancy had pulled a plastic cased tape measure out of her pocket, the kind that rolls up. Her mom had gotten it at a trade show. Ironically, it was an advertisement for Arritane Industries.

"That'll do!" said Nathan.

He explained his plan as we carefully moved the heavy metal bench in the tiny cage over behind the robots that stood perfectly still. The evil scientist had told them not to move and, luckily, they didn't.

Then, with two of us on each side, we threaded the rope through the bars above their heads and watched as Mick silently counted to three. We immediately lowered our ropes over the heads of the robots and pulled as tightly as we could! The most horrifying thing we could ever imagine happened! Instead of them gasping for air…their heads just formed into balls and bounced on the floor!

Chapter Twelve - Sci Fi

It was the freakiest thing! It took all of my concentration to unlock the cage. Because their bodies quickly began searching for their heads…but where their heads had popped off their bodies, it just sealed right up! Almost like they were made solely of liquid and refilled themselves!

"Ooouuuuu!" squealed Sissy!

"Hurry, Mick!" yelled Nathan, as I frantically worked the lock while one of the heads rolled next to the cage as we kicked it away! The bodies couldn't see, so they just searched around the ground with their hands…headless!!!

"I got it!" I screamed as the cage door flew open.

We ran to the door and commanded it to open while the nasty robots were still feeling around for their heads!

It wouldn't open!

Nathan ran hurriedly around the lab, gathering up a timer, some wire, a fuse, other gadgets and equipment.

"Somebody give me some chewed gum!" he said.

"Ouuu…but whatever," exclaimed Sissy, as she pulled out a piece of bubble gum from her pocket, chewed it as fast as she could, then handed the gooey blob to Nathan. He worked quickly, as he wired the door with the gum.

"Okay, I'm ready! Face the other way!" he said, as he pushed a button. Sparks flew, but the door opened instantly!

"This way!" yelled Sissy.

"No, this way!" I yelled and pointed.

We took off running down the long corridor. Once again it was totally freaky and it felt like we were going in circles! There were no signs and only a few doors.

We were afraid to try the doors because 'what if we opened the wrong one?'...

"This has got to be it, right here, before the hallway goes into another long curve!" I screamed.

I held my breath as I tapped it four times in a circle just like the robots did.

It opened and we were instantly amazed! It was like a complete underwater docking station! It was all metal and in the middle, completely covered in water, was a Champ! But not a real Champ...the fake metal Champ!

Chapter Thirteen - Sci Fi

It looked so real that we realized this was the one we had been fighting in the water. The one we thought was real! It looked like it had real dinosaur-like skin over metal…but it was really a submarine!

We ran down the long skinny clear tube into it. The door automatically opened as we jumped in and it shut!

"Great, whose gonna drive this thing?" asked Sissy.

"I am!" said Nancy.

"Whaa…" I said, as we turned to look at her.

"It's like a boat, trust me," said Nancy, "buckle up!"

The submarine was amazing…it had hundreds of controls and gears! We quickly grabbed seats and strapped ourselves in. Nancy then started pushing all kinds of buttons and the strange underwater vehicle made weird moaning sounds, then lurched forward!

They were the same freakish Champ sounds we heard when we were being attacked by it! Now, we knew that Nancy knew a lot more than she was letting on…but this was not the time to ask!

"Okay, we just have to make one more stop!" Nancy explained.

"What? Where?" I asked, while Nathan nodded quietly and Sissy's eyes grew huge as we watched the lake outside the strange submarine on a giant screen fly by!

Nancy made a huge turn as we all held on tightly! Those pods, the minute he finds out we escaped, he will deploy them and they will wipe out the entire eastern seaboard's water source! Not to mention the after effect – once it soaks into the soil!

"Nancy's right," said Nathan, as he took out his notepad. "By my calculations…that liquid is enough to wipe out millions of people! But we can transport it! *We held our breath as we could now see we were heading straight for the glowing purple pods!*

Chapter Fourteen - Sci Fi

Within seconds, Nancy had the ship hovering right above the dangerous liquid! We knew this was going to be a delicate operation, but we had no other choice!

She explained what we had to do as we unbuckled and Nathan and I put on scuba gear…we were going to have to go out and guide the pods into the ship, while Nancy held the submarine steady, and Sissy worked the controls to the decompression chamber.

If it worked, we would save everyone; if it didn't, well, we would all be history.

Nancy went back and steadied the ship. We went into the chamber. Sissy could watch us on a small video screen; we gave her the thumbs up and within seconds were in the water!

Nathan and I were lucky we took swimming and scuba lessons, because this was no easy task! The minute we were in the water we found ourselves fighting a current, but luckily Nancy saw and moved the ship to block us. One by one we turned the giant glass pods to loosen them and then guided them up into the belly of the submarine.

Sissy would open and close the strong metal hatch, then guide them up into a landing place that had specially-sized holders.

We had gotten four and had one more to go…but we were startled when we saw the mad scientist come into his lab and see what had happened. Then he saw us through the window!

We were so shocked at seeing him, we let go of the last pod and it began rising up…we began to swim up to try to catch it!

"NOOOO!" screamed Nancy through the speakers in our head gear!

So, we quickly swam back to the ship and boarded.

"Where did you two go? I freaked out when I couldn't see you on the screen!" cried Sissy.

"We lost one!" I said, catching my breath as I removed my breathing apparatus.

"Well, we almost lost you two!" yelled Sissy.

"Let's go! No time…he's onto us!" screamed Nancy through the speaker.

We helped Sissy finish strapping in the toxic pods. Then we began to climb out of the chamber. Once inside the main area of the ship, we buckled in again…except coming straight for us in a smaller submarine was the madman!

He was shooting large electrical rays at the ship! Nancy turned and dove down, then up again to avoid being hit! It knocked out one of the lights and now the lake was looking blacker than ever!

"To the left!" Nathan screamed as he saw a cave!

"No, he knows every cavern in this lake…we would get trapped! Besides, I have got to get that other container! Hold on!" Nancy yelled, as she turned the sub practically sideways.

He was hot on our trail! But we were a decent distance ahead of him.

"There it is!" I screamed, as I called out nautical directions from the telescope. When she was right near the pod, she gave us directions on how to blast out a net from the side of the ship. On the count of three, we all pushed a massive button and the ship jerked backwards.

I looked out of a scope and could see we caught it! Then, we all turned a huge metal knob to pull it in as close and tightly to the sub as we could. We used every bit of our strength to turn it!

"Hurry!" screamed Nathan, and we could see the mad scientist was coming straight toward our ship!

"Buckle up! Quick!" Nancy screamed, and the next thing we knew was the sub propelled like a rocket straight up in the air!

Seconds later, we were on the surface of the lake. We could see the pod was still with us, and thankfully intact! We were heading straight for the shore at rocket speed!

Lights started flashing red as a voice came over the loudspeaker… "Warning, warning, you are now 100 feet from the shore…99 feet from the shore…98 feet from the shore…"

As the voice continued, we began to brace ourselves.

"We're gonna crash!" yelled Sissy.

"Nancy, what about the liquid?" asked Nathan.

"I'm braking! But it's not slowing down!" screamed Nancy.

"He has control of the ship from his sub!" I yelled, as I could read on the panel a flashing notation that said:

Circuit Override…Circuit Override…

"You are going to have to make a turn, and now!" yelled Nathan.

I quickly leaned over and pulled on the steering wheel, helping Nancy turn the ship!

Now, we were riding sideways along the shore, but at the same top speed!

Nathan had unbuckled and quickly took off a door at the main computer terminal. He was playing with wires and disconnecting things.

"I think I got it!" he said.

But, it was too late…the mad scientist was right along the side of us trying to hit the container!

"Take it back down!" I screamed at the top of my lungs, "it will buy us some time!"

"Mick's right!" yelled Nathan. "The sub is faster and more in control under water.

"Brace yourself!" hollered Nancy.

Within seconds, we were submerged back under water. We could see we managed to shake him!

"It says circuit disengaged! Nathan, you did it!" I squealed at the top of my lungs. "Take her around again!"

Nancy turned the giant Champ submarine around one last time. Again, she blasted it straight up out of the water toward land. This time we were in control! We were heading straight for land while Nancy pulled back on the throttle and we safely landed on shore!

We quickly unbuckled and headed for the door! When we jumped out we were shocked to see there was no crowd, no one running toward us, not a soul in sight!

We ran up the bluff and slowly people began to poke their heads out! Everyone had been hiding, thinking the sub was a real Champ!

Within seconds, everyone came running toward us screaming!

"Mick!!! Are you alright? What's going on?" cried Mom.

"We began to explain as our parents, the crew and everybody surrounded us. We led them back down to the Champ sub; talking to the police, while the Coast Guard arrived. They cut the pod out of the net and began combing the Champ submarine, while the Coast Guard issued a massive search party of boats out into the lake.

Nancy was busy with the police and her family; while we told the story to our family and the crew. By now, the newspaper and television stations were everywhere!

After hours of being interviewed and interrogated, Mr. LaFave had the mess hall set up with dinner for us. We piled our plates with food...we were so happy to be able get something to eat!

"Nancy, how did you know how to drive..." I began, until she quickly interrupted me.

"Oh, isn't this food delicious!" she said, as she glanced toward her mother then looked me straight in the eyes, as if to say 'not now!'

When we finished eating, the four of us managed to get away from the craziness and just sit and talk.

"Well, c'mon spill the beans!" said Sissy.

We waited in anticipation, as Nancy choked out the words..."He...w...was my gran...grandfather."

Chapter Seventeen - Sci Fi

We couldn't believe our ears!

"What? Who?" asked Nathan.

"The madman, the crazy scientist…" Nancy continued. "He was a chemist at the plant and the man who developed the shield. He was up for a Nobel Peace Prize. But then something went wrong in the final stages. They – the owners and managers of the company – wouldn't listen to him. We never knew what happened to him…he just vanished. We had an idea, but we were never sure. He used to tell me stories about Champ when I was young."

"You've got to be kidding!" exclaimed Sissy.

"I wish I was…he had that old submarine for years – I knew it as a regular sub, before he made it up to look like Champ. This was all before he disappeared. When I was young, he would take me exploring the lake in it! He even taught me how to drive it when we would go out on Champ expeditions…I guess he thought he could frighten people off the lake if it looked like Champ…"

Our discussion was broken up when Mom came running over to tell us they had caught him and they were taking him in. Nancy was quickly joined by her family and waved goodbye. We said we would meet up with her later. As she walked away, she was comforted by her parents.

"I'm sure glad my grandfather was a hairdresser!" said Sissy, as Nathan and I just rolled our eyes!

The Submerged Ending

Instant Message Ending

To look up the Instant Message (IM) shortcuts, go to the KEY at the end of the chat session!

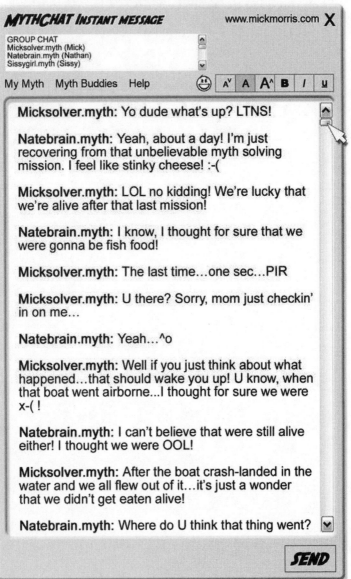

MYTHCHAT INSTANT MESSAGE   www.mickmorris.com **X**

GROUP CHAT
Micksolver.myth (Mick)
Natebrain.myth (Nathan)
Sissygirl.myth (Sissy)

My Myth   Myth Buddies   Help   Aᵛ A Aᶺ **B** *I* u̲

Micksolver.myth: Yo dude what's up? LTNS!

Natebrain.myth: Yeah, about a day! I'm just recovering from that unbelievable myth solving mission. I feel like stinky cheese! :-(

Micksolver.myth: LOL no kidding! We're lucky that we're alive after that last mission!

Natebrain.myth: I know, I thought for sure that we were gonna be fish food!

Micksolver.myth: The last time...one sec...PIR

Micksolver.myth: U there? Sorry, mom just checkin' in on me...

Natebrain.myth: Yeah...^o

Micksolver.myth: Well if you just think about what happened...that should wake you up! U know, when that boat went airborne...I thought for sure we were x-(!

Natebrain.myth: I can't believe that were still alive either! I thought we were OOL!

Micksolver.myth: After the boat crash-landed in the water and we all flew out of it...it's just a wonder that we didn't get eaten alive!

Natebrain.myth: Where do U think that thing went?

SEND

194

MYTHCHAT *INSTANT MESSAGE*   www.mickmorris.com X

GROUP CHAT
Micksolver.myth (Mick)
Natebrain.myth (Nathan)
Sissygirl.myth (Sissy)

My Myth   Myth Buddies   Help   ☺ A⌄ A A∧ **B** *I* u̲

Micksolver.myth: I don't know. I was just thankful that we all got back on the boat! Well look who just signed on. :-(

Sissygirl.myth: Hi guys! HAY? What's up?

Micksolver.myth: Hey Sissy.

Natebrain.myth: Hi Sissy.

Sissygirl.myth: Has anyone heard from Nancy?

Micksolver.myth: No.

Natebrain.myth: Me neither.

Sissygirl.myth: OIC...

Micksolver.myth: We were just chatting about that last mission and how it was a really close call...especially after the boat tipped over. I wonder if that big chunk of Champ that the engine sliced out of him, killed him?

Sissygirl.myth: FWIW I almost gag every time I think about that big, bleeding mess of black grossness!

Micksolver.myth: LU

Sissygirl.myth: Oh, like it didn't bother you! :-O

Natebrain.myth: I think what Mick is trying to say is that there was more to think about than the chunk of Champ.

SEND

GROUP CHAT
Micksolver.myth (Mick)
Natebrain.myth (Nathan)
Sissygirl.myth (Sissy)

My Myth   Myth Buddies   Help   😊   Aᵛ A Aᶺ **B** *I* <u>u</u>

Natebrain.myth: Like next time we have to be more cautious when...

Sissygirl.myth: Yeah...I know and my problem is my mom keeps asking me questions like why the Coast Guard had to rescue us from the lake!

Micksolver.myth: Sissy KYMS!

Natebrain.myth: Sissy you have to KYMS!

Micksolver.myth: LOL GMTA

Natebrain.myth: :-D

Sissygirl.myth: Maybe B4 I wouldn't have thought about telling her...but FWIW you two should know by now that I will keep it to myself! What will it take for me to prove myself as a myth solver?

Micksolver.myth: uh...

Sissygirl.myth: Didn't I help slap that thing with the oars after we got back in the boat? In fact wasn't I the one who managed to clobber it right in the face????

Natebrain.myth: SRY

Sissygirl.myth: ...while its nasty big teeth were just about to bite my head off! Huh? Huh? So what am I FOF? I need to know right now! >:-(

                                                      SEND

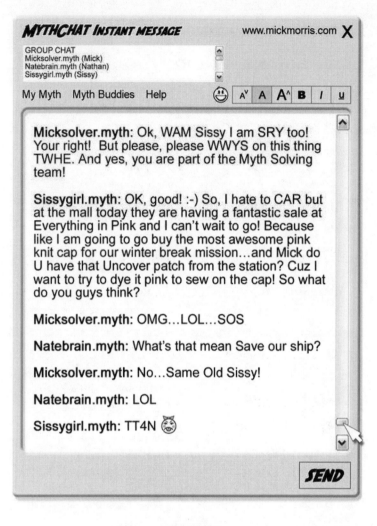

MYTHCHAT *INSTANT MESSAGE*   www.mickmorris.com **X**

GROUP CHAT
Micksolver.myth (Mick)
Natebrain.myth (Nathan)
Sissygirl.myth (Sissy)

My Myth   Myth Buddies   Help   ☺   Aᵛ A Aᴬ **B** *I* <u>u</u>

Micksolver.myth: Ok, WAM Sissy I am SRY too! Your right! But please, please WWYS on this thing TWHE. And yes, you are part of the Myth Solving team!

Sissygirl.myth: OK, good! :-) So, I hate to CAR but at the mall today they are having a fantastic sale at Everything in Pink and I can't wait to go! Because like I am going to go buy the most awesome pink knit cap for our winter break mission...and Mick do U have that Uncover patch from the station? Cuz I want to try to dye it pink to sew on the cap! So what do you guys think?

Micksolver.myth: OMG...LOL...SOS

Natebrain.myth: What's that mean Save our ship?

Micksolver.myth: No...Same Old Sissy!

Natebrain.myth: LOL

Sissygirl.myth: TT4N 🐷

SEND

L8R

Instant Message KEY

My Myth   Myth Buddies   Help   😃 Aᵛ A Aᴧ **B** *I* u̲

Internet Chat KEY

B4: Before

CAR: Chat and Run

FOF: Friend or Foe

FWIW: For Whatever It's Worth

GMTA: Great Minds Think Alike

HAY: How Are You?

KYMS: Keep Your Mouth Shut

L8R: Later

LOL: Laugh Out Loud

LU: Lighten Up

LTNS: Long Time No See

OIC: Oh I See

OMG: Oh My Gosh

OOL: Out of Luck

PIR: Parents in Room

SOS: Save Our Ship or Same Old Sissy

TT4N: Ta Ta For Now

TWHE: The Walls Have Ears

U: You

WAM: Wait a Minute

WWYS: Watch What You Say

:-)   Smiling

:-D   Laughing

>:-(Upset or annoyed

:-O   Shouting loudly

:-(Frowning

x-(Dead

^o   Snoring

END

198

Quebec

The Lake
Champlain Basin

New York

Lake Champlain and Champ Facts

Lake Champlain is located between upper New York and Vermont, extending into Quebec. The lake is 125 miles long and 400 feet deep.

Champ, the myth of Lake Champlain, first began by Native American tribes who were said to celebrate the lake monsters existence. Then in 1609 French explorer Samuel de Champlain who discovered the lake, claimed that he had spotted the creature while in battle with the Iroquois on the bank of the lake.

Champ is said to be a giant type of serpent that lives in Lake Champlain.

There have been 240 sightings recorded. Port Henry, New York has a Champ statue and Champ Day on the first Saturday in August.

Champ is frequently compared to the Loch Ness monster because of the similarities of the lakes. Scientists have said that Champ and the Loch Ness could both possibly be plesiosaurs, 25-30 feet long with extremely long necks. Both lakes are extremely long and over 300 feet deep. Both lakes formed after the Ice Age.

Port Henry

Vermont

Laws have now been passed to protect Champ and it has been given the scientific name of Champtanystropeus.

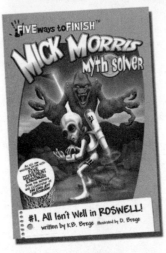

About the Breges

Author Karen Bell-Brege just so happens to be married to the illustrator, Darrin M. Brege. This is their fourth book together, and their third in the bestselling *Mick Morris Myth Solver* series with *Five Ways to Finish*.

Karen is a comic and a speaker, as well as the director of an improv comedy troupe. Darrin is also a comic, and a radio personality. He has created tons of illustrations for national companies, as well as picture books. He is also the original cover artist that branded the Michigan and American Chillers series.

The Brege's have one son – whose name as if it is any surprise is Mick! They live in a funky, old townhouse in the Midwest and they love to laugh and have fun! On rainy nights they have a blast making up crazy, scary stories!

Would you like the Breges to visit your school? They have an awesome presentation that will keep you laughing while you learn about art, writing, and reading!

Just have your teacher or school administrator contact their office at (248) 890-5363 for more information on their special presentation!

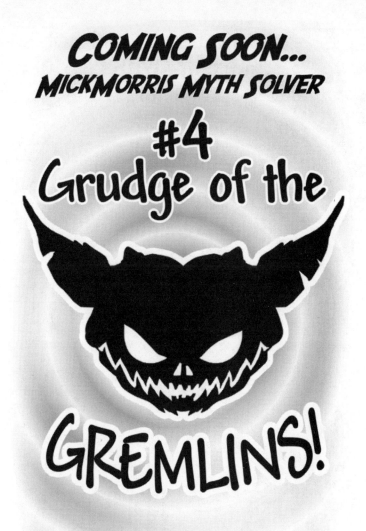

COMING SOON...
MICKMORRIS MYTH SOLVER

#4
Grudge of the

GREMLINS!